LET THE WILLOWS WEEP

LET THE
WILLOWS
WEEP

SHERRY PARNELL

Publisher's Cataloging-in-Publication Data

Names: Parnell, Sherry, author.
Title: Let the willows weep / Sherry Parnell.
Description: Glenmoore, PA: Sherry Parnell, 2019.
Identifiers: ISBN 978-1-7333077-0-3 (pbk.) | 978-1-7333077-1-0
(ebook)
Subjects: LCSH Southern states--Fiction. | Family--Fiction. |
Girls--Fiction. | Women--Southern States--Fiction. | Coming
of age--Fiction. | Bildungsroman. | Historical fiction. | BISAC
FICTION / Southern | FICTION / Small Town & Rural |
FICTION / Literary
Classification: LCC PS3616.A7625 L48 2019| DDC 813.6--dc23

Library of Congress Control Number: 2019915418

ISBN 978-1-7333077-0-3

For my husband, Rick Parnell
Love of my life, keeper of my dreams

And
For my parents, with love

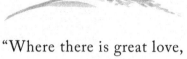

"Where there is great love,
there are always miracles."

—Willa Cather

PART I

CHAPTER
ONE

The day he left was the day I swallowed red. I know it was red because that is the color of rage and shame. I was to learn, though, that it is also the color of passion and love.

I could understand why my father would leave my mother, but me? I wasn't like her at all. She was long and gaunt, stretched like a worn rubber band. Her skin was no longer pink but sallow like the underside of a chicken's wrinkled throat. With her voice long hardened from smoking Kent cigarettes, she spat out commands and insults that tore at your heart. I guess my father left before there was nothing left of his.

My sense of being seeped through the wooden slats when he walked off the porch, as if all that was me was contained in the soles of his shoes. The battered screen door slammed against its frame, cracking the silence of the kitchen. She grimaced in pain, saying the noise hurt her ears. I guess it takes less pride for your ears to hurt than your heart but mine was shattered and my hatred for her grew in between every crevice.

He was gone in a slam of a door and the start of a coughing engine. The spinning tires swirled the dust into tiny tornados. I wanted to run, jump inside the car, and beg him to take me with him. Fearing he would look at me and only see her, I sat still and waited.

Motionless on the hard wooden chair with my bare legs tucked under the rungs, I tried to avoid the splinters as I wiped away the sweat that trickled down my forehead along with the tears that flowed down my cheeks. The heat bore heavy on my chest and my legs became leaden as I drifted into a restless sleep.

Dawn crept through the window. Streams of light streaked the linoleum floor, showing the yellow stains and deep cuts where dirt had settled into the grooves. I watched as morning slowly swallowed the remaining night. My head lay on the table. I didn't want to move my face from its cool spot, but my neck started to tighten and ache. I stood and shook sleep from my tired arms and legs.

Through watery eyes, I squinted as the morning sunlight spilled into the room.

I looked out the window to see the sun scorch the edges of the milky clouds in a burnt red. The color was brilliant and warm, so unlike the coldness that had settled into my bones since my father left.

I longed to feel that warmth inside of me, so I stood as tall as I could, which only amounted to about four feet and eleven inches if I really stretched, and opened my mouth. I imagined the sun's furious red color slipping past my blistered lips, across my dry tongue, and down my throat. I then slumped onto the floor and prayed for the color to fill the emptiness inside of me.

"Stand up! I haven't scrubbed the floor yet, and now I have a dress to clean," she bellowed, startling me. I quickly stood and turned to face her. She appeared as she had yesterday and the day before that. He left and it was as though everything was unaffected except that my heart was broken and hers had only hardened more.

She went to the sink and began to wash last night's supper dishes, which had been left in the commotion of yesterday's events. It was the only evidence that our life had been interrupted. "They aren't going to dry themselves," she said as she threw a dish towel at me.

I slowly stumbled over to the dry board and picked up a dish. The indigo pattern was faded and the edges were laced with tiny cracks and chips, a spiderweb story of sparse dinners and many washings.

After the dishes were done, I remained in my spot watching her dry her hands on her worn apron. As she turned to leave the kitchen, I asked, "Is he going to come home...?" My voice trailed off, leaving the words alone in the thick, humid air. She spun around on her heel, her eyes like little shards of glass piercing into me.

Stammering, I tried again. "I just mean...should I..."

My words faltered as she coldly stared at me. "Don't ask stupid questions. There is nothing you can do. If he left then he's gone." I dropped my head. My mother tilted my chin toward her with the crook of her finger and said more softly, "In my experience, child, those who leave with only their back facing you aren't coming home." These were the only words of comfort she offered before turning and leaving me once more alone. I swallowed hard, fighting back the tears and the urge to scream.

The following weeks passed slowly. As the days wore on, each became hotter than the last. It was soon the time of the year when the comfort of coolness is sought but rarely found. My mother spent her days locked in her room with a metal fan and an overflowing ashtray. I sought my own refuge in a secret place I discovered in the woods behind our house. It became my sanctuary and its peace, my long desired friend.

The spot was located by a small stream, which had dried up in the long months of heat and little rain, showing its cracked and dirty underbelly. A tree had fallen in one of the storms and lay bent over the streambed with gnarled limbs and twigs that jutted out like fingers.

I comfortably lay on a smooth spot of the trunk daydreaming until I heard her shriek my name. The sound seemed to bounce off of every tree, echoing my name over and over again. Panicked, I slipped as I clumsily tried to unwind my legs from the tree. I quickly pulled myself up and ran as fast as I could, stumbling over brambles and jumping over bushes in a race to reach the house before she shouted my name again.

As I neared the clearing with the yard in sight, I saw her standing with her back stiffened and her jaw clenched. I moved toward her slowly with my head lowered. She grabbed the sleeve of my T-shirt and pulled the material tight as she roughly brushed the dirt from my shoulder.

Out of the corner of my eye, I watched her hands. I had seen them many times as she washed dishes, pulled them from scrub buckets, or pointed a warning finger at me. It was only now, however, that I truly became aware of them. Her slender and delicate fingers with tiny veins that loomed beneath her skin in blue and purple attire bearing witness to the flow of blood and strength to her limbs. Her nails kept short for practicality were also kept clean and shiny with a glossy purplish hue. Her hands, I decided, were a part of her beauty that still remained.

Pulling my own hand from my pocket I lightly touched her fingers. She flinched and pulled away. She then turned her hand from front to back as if she too were surprised at what she found attached to her bony limbs. I raised my head and looked into her eyes, trembling slightly from my bold action and the rare occasion in which it occurred.

Red-rimmed and slowly filling with tears, her eyes became vacant as they so often did lately. I pushed my hand back into my pocket and said nothing, knowing that my mother was again lost in her memories.

TWO

A small tear fell onto the back of my hand with a muted drop, but it struck my heart with a loud remembrance of a time nearly forgotten. Swept back into my memories, I no longer saw my daughter, mud-stained and timid, standing before me. Instead I saw the family that had left me long before my husband did.

Ten years old and small I could easily stay out of sight. Today I crouched beside the porch, poking at ants as I listened to my brothers talking. Most of what they said was about my fight with Billy Hawkins. Billy was in my grade, but he was twice the size of the rest of the kids. My mother says it is because he is from large stock, but I figured it was because Billy had been in fourth grade longer than the schoolhouse had been standing.

The fight was nothing more than a push, a punch, and a scolding, but it proved to be a source of my brothers' amusement and my mother's disappointment for days. I told everyone that Billy had pushed me, but the truth was he was making fun of me again. He'd taking to calling me "peacock," saying that I strutted around showing off my feathers like I thought I was so pretty. Mostly I could ignore him, but on that day I couldn't watch his plump lips spray spit into the air as he clucked and cackled. I didn't even notice that my hand had clenched into a tight ball and left my side until I saw it make contact with Billy's cheek.

I was happy that my punch shut Billy up, but impressing my older brother Denny was my real win. Denny never missed a chance to tell the story, giving new details and exaggerating the wounds, and I never missed the chance to listen, feeling good in his pride.

Denny sat down on the large stump in our yard just close enough for me to hear him say, "Come on, Caul, you got to admit she's tough." Denny was my constant defender even to my other brother, Caul, who took every chance to find some fault in me.

Caul slumped down onto the grass next to him and hissed, "I don't have to admit nothing. She got in a lucky punch. That don't make her tough. It makes her lucky."

Denny shook his head. "You're jealous."

From over the railing, I saw Caul jump up so he faced Denny before he spit out, "I am not! She's just always in the way."

Denny grinned and said, "Well, I think she was exactly where she needed to be when she landed that right hook to Billy's cheek."

Caul rolled his eyes and stomped toward the house.

And that's the way it was with my older brothers. Denny my fierce protector and Caul my constant rival. It's easy to love Denny because he had always loved me so much but everything with Caul was uneasy.

I was squatted down beneath the slats of the porch, so Caul didn't see me as he tramped up the steps but Mother did. "What are you doing?" she shrieked at me. Taking three quick steps down the porch, she screeched, "Look at you!" I looked down to see that my knees were sunk deep in mud. Mother roughly grabbed my arm and pulled me up. "I was going to invite some of the ladies over for tea, but how would that look for them to see my daughter covered in filth?"

I shrugged. Mother huffed in disgust.

She tightened her grasp on my arm, and I knew she wanted an answer. What answer could I give when Mother always made tea for ladies who never came no matter how many smudge marks were on my worn cotton dress? Denny said that Mother was trying to give us a better life, but I thought she just wanted a better one for herself so she pretended the one we lived didn't exist.

I let out a small cry as Mother squeezed my arm tighter. Squirming away from her, I saw Denny running toward us. Breathless and red-faced, he put his hand on her arm and said, "Mother?"

Startled by Denny's touch, Mother let go of me and turned to him. "Oh, darling, I didn't see you."

Denny said, "Mother, I was thinking I could clear the wood in the back lot before Daddy gets home, but it would be easier if Birddog helped me load the wagon."

Denny had called me Birddog for so long that it felt more like my name than my given one. He once told me that he picked it because I was tiny like a little bird but strong and loyal as a dog. I liked it.

Mother looked into Denny's eyes for a bit before her lips curled, like a fat tabby's tail, into a smile. "Sure, son, that sounds good," she said while staring at me disapprovingly. Grateful she agreed, I straightened my dress and grabbed Denny's arm. Of course, I knew she would. She always did when it's Denny doing the asking. After all, Mother thought the sun rose on Denny's shoulders. I might not have agreed with a lot of what she thought, but that's one I couldn't argue.

Denny and I had only taken a few steps before Mother called out, "Don't overwork yourself, dear. The wood will still be there tomorrow." Lowering her voice, she said to me, "Don't get in the way. Help when you can and sit still when you can't." Sighing, she added, "I guess we'll worry about getting your nails clean later." Denny grabbed my hand and as he pulled me toward the wood cart, I looked back to see Mother watching us. How odd, I thought, that she could feel so much pride for one child and so much spite for another.

"Come on, Birddog, don't you worry about Mother. She'll forget all about your nails when she sees how many carts of wood you can pull." Denny tried to make me feel better by acting as if it was only my dirty nails that made Mother angry with me, but we both knew that it was much more than that.

I shoved my hands into my pockets and plodded behind Denny. Turning to look at me, he said, "You ain't going to get much done that way." I slowly pulled my hands free and smiled weakly. Denny stopped and said, "Birddog. She don't mean it. She just…worries too much."

I shrugged.

Denny said, "You can start by the field. Load up as many pieces of wood as you can without tipping the cart." I nodded. Denny added, "You're a good kid, Birddog." I smiled.

Denny's kind words muted my mother's harsh ones. As I headed toward the edge of our yard, I felt loved. And in that moment, I couldn't imagine a time when he wouldn't be able to always make me feel that way.

For two hours, Denny and I lifted and loaded wood. We pulled the full carts to the woodshed to be piled in a neatly arranged triangle. I worked until my arms ached and my back tightened from bending and twisting. I was tired and thirsty, but I didn't quit. I wanted Denny and my daddy to be proud of the work I'd done, and I guess some small part of me also hoped that Mother would be pleased.

Sweat trickled down my temple. Reaching up to brush back the hairs that had come loose from my ribbon, I looked across the lawn and saw Daddy. The thick, moist air made a haze that settled around Daddy as he shuffled toward us, making him look more like a ghost than a man.

As he neared us, Daddy became not much more than the whites of his eyes as the rest of him disappeared beneath the thick black soot of the mines. He moved toward Denny first. Slapping him playfully on the back, Daddy said, "You sure saved me a sore back and lots of time." Always willing to share the praise, Denny said, "I didn't do it alone. Birddog lifted and carted as much wood as I did."

Daddy gently squeezed my shoulder and said, "I don't doubt it a bit." Then leaning down, he whispered, "I'm real proud of you." As Daddy withdrew his hand, his beaming gaze was broken by Mother's voice calling us in for supper.

She stood in the doorway bathed in the purples and pinks of early twilight, giving her the glow of an angel. Her hair, which was shiny as silk and the color of cinnamon sticks, was neatly piled atop her head. A few strands fell and curled around her face, barely brushing her delicate pale skin. Her slender arms were crossed and resting on her breast as she leaned against the wooden door frame impatiently waiting for us. Although the words that slipped past Mother's tongue weren't always pretty, her beauty couldn't be denied.

The thick, still air smothered any coolness, but as if even the breeze couldn't resist being near her, it danced around her legs, gracefully shifting her soft cotton dress into gentle folds. Mother wore her cornflower-blue dress. I knew she'd picked it because it made her eyes brighter than a summer day.

I watched Daddy, with his face covered in soot and his back stooped from long days, stare at my mother with her polished skin standing in her pressed dress. I wondered if there had been a time when Daddy's hands were white and clean and if Mother had believed they would always stay that way.

Breaking our silent stares, Daddy said, "Well, we better wash up and head in for supper. We don't want a hot meal going cold on account of us." He reached for my hand as he nudged Denny ahead of us. Slowly, Daddy let out a deep breath and upon it he whispered, "She sure is beautiful." Daddy said that we all had something in life that we held dear. It's just a pity that Mother chose to cherish something that faded faster than a firefly's light.

CHAPTER
THREE

The kitchen was warm from the afternoon sun and the heat of the cook stove. The sweet smell of buttered cornbread floated through the air causing my mouth to water. I took my seat between Denny and Mother and eagerly watched as the bowls were placed on the table.

I leaned over the bowl of green beans until I could feel the steam sweep across my forehead. Mother scolded, "Lean back and sit in your chair like a proper lady. We haven't even said grace." She then shoved a large serving spoon into the dish, twisting her elbow toward me so that I had to duck out of her way.

After she placed the last bowl onto the table, Mother sat and reached her hands toward mine. Grace was the one time that I actually got to slip my hand inside of my mother's. Even after all of the times that we said grace at this table, I was still always surprised at the coolness of her touch.

We bowed our heads and Mother began the prayer. "We thank you, dear Father, for the bounty you've placed before us and for the health of our family. Thank you also, Lord, for our dutiful sons. In Jesus's—"

Daddy quickly cut in, adding, "And we thank you, Lord, for our daughter, who is hardworking and loving."

I could feel Mother's hand tighten around mine as she mumbled, "Of course. In Jesus's name, amen." She shook loose my hand before the word *amen* had crossed her lips. I didn't mind that Mother forgot me in the prayer because I knew that God wouldn't. Or at least I hoped.

I slowly looked up to see Daddy watching me. He tilted his head slightly and smiled. My throat tightened and my eyes tingled with the threat of tears not because Mother had again forgotten me but because of Daddy's sad smile— part love, part pity. I quickly looked at my plate and prayed, *Please, God, if you can't make me what she wants then please make her want what I already am.*

My thoughts drifted but were broken by the sound of spoons clinking against bowls and glasses being bumped into plates. I sat quietly with my legs crossed underneath me, hoping that the height it gave me would make me seem bigger than I felt at that moment.

Mother grabbed the serving spoon and ladled lumps of mashed potatoes onto each of our plates. "I wish I could give you boys more than one scoop, but this is it." She sighed.

Seeing Daddy's shoulders slump, Denny quickly said, "I'm not very hungry."

Giving Daddy a sideways glance, Mother said, "Growing boys need food."

Mother abruptly sat up and spooned a few pieces of peaches into her mouth. Swallowing hard, she set down her spoon and said sharply, "I have come to accept chipped plates..." Studying her spoon, she added, "And tarnished silverware, but it is not acceptable for our children to be hungry."

Denny set down his own spoon and argued, "Mother, we are not going hungry." Rare to do so, Mother ignored Denny as she looked at my father for an answer.

With his head lowered, Daddy mumbled, "The foreman told me today that because Boney quit, he needs the back tunnel covered. So, I'm going take on those hours."

Mother shrugged and said, "If you think that will help."

Daddy scooped his remaining peas onto Caul's plate and said, "I think every little bit helps."

I watched Mother as she angrily dug her fork into her chicken and snapped, "Very little."

Always patient, Daddy gently pushed back his plate, leaned closer to Mother, and asked, "What's wrong?"

With a forced smile, Mother said, "Nothing. It's just been a long day."

All Mother's days seemed long, filled with hours that slowly crept by crowded with dirty washing and meals that seemed to begin as soon as the last dish was cleaned. She'd done these daily tasks so many times that the purpose had faded leaving only a habit. At the end of her day, all she was left with were the complaints she piled upon Daddy's already tired back like bags on a pack mule. He always listened, promising her that everything would get better, which pleased her but only for a moment.

Caul spent most of his time during dinner making tunnels in his mashed potatoes. Smearing the last bit across his plate, he excitedly asked Daddy, "When do I get to be a mole man?"

Daddy cupped his hand over Caul's shoulder and said, "If I can help it, son, never."

Smushing the potato tunnels flat, Caul groaned and asked, "Why?"

Daddy said, "It's not where I want my boys to be." Quickly looking at Mother, he added, "It don't make for a good life."

The men who worked in the mines were called moles because they spent most of their time underground in the dark, scurrying around in the small and dirty cracks of the earth. Instead of breathing in fresh air and feeling the warmth of the sun, they breathed in soot and feared cave-ins. My father was nothing like a little blind rat, though. After he shook off the dirt of the day, all that remained was a strong man whose only blindness was to my mother.

It's not often quiet during dinner, but when it was I knew it wouldn't be long before Mother turned her attention and anger toward me. Shoving back her plate, Mother looked at Daddy and demanded, "Do you know what really made today hard?" It took no more than his raised eyebrows for her to go on.

Pointing at me, she hissed, "She did it again."

Daddy asked, "Did what?"

Mother shook her head and nearly shouted, "She disobeyed me! Again. I've repeatedly told her that I don't want her getting muddy and playing with dirty little bugs but does she listen?"

Never really wanting an answer to her question, Mother said, "How is she ever going to be a part of respectable society when she is always up to her elbows in grime?" Just getting started, Mother took a deep breath and said, "She needs discipline. You need to discipline her and I think—"

Daddy cut in, "Wait a minute. You need to slow down. First of all, I ain't going to correct the child for getting dirty because that's what kids do." Stopping, he looked at me and said, "You're a good girl and as long as you do what is right and stay true to yourself then you'll always be respectable."

Daddy again turned to Mother and said, "Second of all, I don't know what society you are talking about, but if it's those few stingy old ladies sitting slurping tea at Vivian's every afternoon then you need to rethink what's important." Not used to Daddy's harshness with her, Mother's back stiffened, but she said nothing. Daddy said, "I know that I don't want our daughter to be a part of a circle of gossips who judge a person's worth by a string of pearls and a diamond brooch."

Mother's face flushed red as she puffed up like a rattler about to strike. "I've heard enough. Those women are not gossiping as you call it. They are talking about important community matters and I see nothing wrong with admiring someone's riches if it has been earned honestly."

Pushing back her chair, Mother stood and said, "I would love the chance to have tea at Vivian's but this is just one more thing not possible on a miner's pay." Daddy's head dropped as Mother stomped down the hall. Mother didn't strike often but when she did she made sure it hurt.

Vivian's Tea Room was in the center of town and was one of the only places that the refined ladies, as Mother called them, could go and enjoy the company of one another. It sat upon the street with a white awning that stretched across the cracked sidewalk and every time I walked underneath I was reminded that some places were there just to let others know that they didn't belong.

When I had to pass by the Tea Room, I straightened my back and quickened my step but there was something about those pink-and-gold-striped wingback chairs and blue china teacups set on white linen napkins that tugged at Mother causing her, I think, to regret some of the choices she had made in her life.

Maybe she blamed Daddy for not making enough money or us for being the extra mouths she had to feed, but I believe you become who you are meant to be. Sometimes you choose your life and other times it chooses you.

I don't really know why Mother wanted so much to be one of those women who only felt important when they made others feel small. Those snobby silver-haired ladies, with thinly lined pink lips and rouge that stuck in the wrinkles of their cheeks, seemed silly in a town where the rich folks were the ones whose house wasn't built on a dirt road marked with potholes and ruts. Their roads were the only ones with signposts. I guess when you have something in life others want to know where to find you.

The rest of us went on unnoticed, hidden away in our small houses with chipped paint and broken shutters, hidden on rough winding roads leading to cornfields and cow pastures and nowhere at all.

CHAPTER

FOUR

Summer slipped into September like sand through my toes. It had been a time when nothing too exciting happened worth adding to my memory and nothing too terrible to try to forget. Sweet days spent drinking iced teas and swimming with Denny were scattered among the sour days spent squabbling with Caul and being scolded by Mother so that all the days went by in a hazy, hot blur.

I didn't mind much that I had to go back to school today since I'd been missing the cool breezes of fall and time away from Mother's watchful eye. I did mind, however, that Denny was going to the upper school this year. Denny leaving earlier meant I was left to bear Caul's teasing alone on the walk to school every morning. I was worried about what Caul aimed to do now that Denny wouldn't be around to protect me. Suddenly shoved into the counter, I turned around to see Caul smirking at me, and then I knew I had every right to worry.

"Move!" Caul hissed as he shoved me onto the porch. Putting my hands out, I was about to shove him when Mother stomped onto the porch, grabbed my arm, and scolded, "Stop it! Wasn't it enough that I had to put up with this all summer?" I tried to wriggle out of Mother's grasp, but she only squeezed tighter and hissed, "There will be no fights this year. You are in fifth grade now. I need you to act like it." Letting go of my arm, she pushed me forward and said, "You mind your brother."

I hurried down the stairs and started across the yard with Caul close at my heels. "Wait up, Dog Face." Knowing Mother was still standing on the porch, I said nothing. Turning the corner of our house, Caul started chanting again, "Dog Face. Dog Face."

Whipping around, I shoved him and shouted, "Stop it, Caul!" He shoved me back and sneered, "I don't have to stop nothing. Mother said you have to mind me." I quickened my pace but Caul kept up, taunting me along the way.

"Minding me means doing everything I say." Caul stopped short, pulled out a piece of onion grass, and stuck it between his teeth. Twirling it between his lips, he poked me in the arm and said, "You hear me?" I didn't answer. "Ain't no Denny around to protect you now, and if you go squealing on me to him I'll make sure you're running to school every day."

Now I stopped short, turned, and balled up my fist. Caul snickered and said, "I'd put that fist back down because I ain't that bully you punched last year." Balling his own fist and putting it right next to my cheek, he hissed, "I hit back."

Caul dropped his arm, and I walked past him. I'd only looked down for a second when I felt a hard shove to my shoulder. Startled, I was knocked off my feet, landing hard on my side. Caul laughed. I rolled slowly over and stood. Stooping down to pick up my spilled lunch, I saw a dark muddy stain on the front of my dress. I tried to rub the spot clean, but I only made it worse.

I groaned thinking about Mother's early morning lecture. She'd warned me not to get dirty. I looked down again at the spot. There was no way I could hide it from her. As I shoved my apple into my lunch bag, something swelled inside of me and slowly dripped down to my hands, curling them into a tight ball. I was no longer afraid. All I felt was rage as I began to run.

I ran so fast that I couldn't feel the ground under my feet. The wind stung my eyes and blew my hair into my mouth, but all I could see was Caul and all I could feel was hatred. As I got closer, I stuck out my arms straight out in front of me with my palms facing forward. Then with all of my force, I smashed into him causing us both to topple to the ground. Having the air knocked out of him, Caul lay facedown in the dirt.

Still angry, I jumped to my feet and barreled on top of him with my fists swinging. Because he started rolling hard from side to side, I couldn't manage a good hit. As I tried to pin his arms with my legs I was pulled up by the back of my dress.

Stumbling to my feet, I turned to see Denny. He reached his hand toward Caul, who batted it away. Slowly standing, Caul headed toward me to get even. Denny pushed him back and said, "Get on to school, Caul." Caul didn't move. Denny pushed harder and said, "Now!"

Before stomping away from us, Caul looked at me and hissed, "He won't always be around to save you, Dog Face."

Brushing the dirt off of my shoulder, Denny asked, "Are you okay, Birddog?" I nodded because I was always okay when Denny was around. "Well then, we should get going before you're really late." Denny started walking.

Looking back at me, he said, "Come on."

I quickly caught up and asked, "Denny, why aren't you at school?"

He smiled and said, "I was but then I got to thinking about you and Caul walking to school together and how a mile is quite a ways for you not to kill him."

I tried to keep from grinning as I said, "I wouldn't have *killed* him."

Denny laughed and said, "Maybe not, but you had a good run at it." I laughed too until I looked down and saw the spot again. I stopped and tried again to clean it, but the stain only darkened and spread.

Seeing my eyes well up, Denny put his arm around me and said softly, "It's okay, Birddog. I'll explain it to Mother." Then, without ever asking what really happened, he grabbed my hand and walked me to school without either of us saying another word. For the rest of the walk, Denny did what he always did—made me feel safe and loved.

Once we reached the brown stone schoolhouse with the black sloping shingles, Denny let go of my hand. Taking out his red handkerchief, he dabbed my cheeks and the top of my forehead then said, "There. Better." Putting the cloth back in his pocket, he said, "I can't go in with you, Birddog, because I am already really late." I nodded and headed toward the door. Turning back again, Denny called out, "I'll come get you after school." Then he gave a quick wave and headed down the road. I took a deep breath and walked toward Ms. Sprigg's fifth-grade class.

As I slowly opened the classroom door, the loud crack of the pointer hitting against her desk caused me to jump. "Well, young lady, being tardy is not a good way to start the year." Ms. Sprigg thwacked the pointer against her palm and said, "Take your seat."

Not knowing where to sit, I stood waiting to be told. Clearly annoyed, Ms. Sprigg said, "I can't have you standing in the middle of the doorway." Rolling her eyes, she asked, "Last name?"

Dropping my head, I mumbled, "Harlin."

Picking up a piece of paper, she made a check and said "Harlin" in a muffled whisper like she was saying a dirty word. Then she said, "We sit alphabetically, so that means you can take your seat next to William Hawkins."

I sat down next to Billy, who grinned and whispered, "Hello, Peacock."

Ms. Sprigg picked up a piece of chalk, cleared her throat, and said, "Well, perhaps now we can begin without any more interruptions." As she wrote a math problem on the board, Billy jabbed his chubby finger into my ribs causing me to yell out. Ms. Sprigg wheeled around and said, "Who was that?" No one answered.

Slowly walking down each aisle, she eyed each one of the students then she turned to me and said, "I trust you won't start any scuffles in my classroom, young lady."

Rubbing my side, I said, "No, ma'am."

I scrunched as far as I could to my side of the bench, but Billy still found a way to push his leg against mine, nearly knocking me off my seat. "Too good to sit next to me, Peacock?" Ignoring him, I opened my notebook. Pulling it away from me, he said, "I ain't giving it back unless you take notes for me too."

In a hushed voice, I snapped, "I ain't doing nothing for you, Billy Hawkins, and you poke me again we are going to have a problem."

Billy leaned in and said, "I'd like to see you try."

Pulling my notebook back, I said, "Didn't you see enough last year?"

Smirking, Billy poked me in the ribs causing me to yell out again.

Ms. Sprigg swung around, set her chalk on her desk, and ordered us to tell her who screamed. Billy again raised his fat finger, but this time he pointed it right at me. The room was so quiet that the clicking of her shoes echoed off of every wall. The clacking sound stopped as she reached my desk.

Slapping her hands down on it, she shoved her face into mine and snapped, "It is clear that you cannot stay composed and sit like a proper young lady, so you will rise from your seat and face the chalkboard for the rest of the day." She turned quickly on her heel, and I slowly followed.

Once I reached the board, Ms. Sprigg grabbed the back of my neck and pushed my nose into the hard slate. Everyone stared at me, making my whole body feel hotter than the fires in Mother's cook stove.

Pulling my shoulders back, Ms. Sprigg snapped, "You don't need to stand that close to the board." Her words were sharp and her tight face held no trace of kindness. Even though the taste of chalk dried my mouth and choked my throat, I didn't move an inch.

Ms. Sprigg scrawled a word across the board in large swooping letters causing the chalk to screech against the slate. Tingles marched across my skin like little ants, but I still didn't budge. Stepping back, she pointed to the word and said, "*Disappointed.* This is the word Ms. Harlin has helped us to learn today." She didn't need to tell me what it meant. I learned it from Mother a long time ago. And as I stood there, alone, I felt it.

At the end of the day, all the students gathered their things, slid off their seats, and headed for home. I still didn't move. As Ms. Sprigg erased the board, she said, "You can go now, young lady." I went to my desk and gathered my books.

Ms. Sprigg pointed to the last word left on the board and said, "Try not to *disappoint* me tomorrow." I wanted to ask how I could disappoint people who didn't seem to have much hope for me anyway. But with my chest tight with tears, I only managed a nod. She also nodded and said, "Go, but I hope to have better days from you." As I walked out the door, I hoped there would be better days *for* me.

CHAPTER
FIVE

I waited for Denny under a big weeping willow tree in the front schoolyard. I stepped into its shade, slumped down, and leaned my head against its smooth trunk. With the limbs bowed down around me, I watched as the breeze wisped the long branches closer to the ground until the tips of the tiny leaves touched the blades of grass. Safely hidden from the other kids jumping rope and playing hopscotch, I felt the tears I'd held back flow down my cheeks.

I sat listening to the thud of stones hitting hopscotch spaces, the soft swishing of ropes brushing over the dirt, and the sounds of giggles and shouts until it all melted into a hushed mumble. My head drooped onto my shoulder and my eyelids became heavy as this playground song hummed in my ear.

I awoke to an empty playground. I stared for a bit, confused, until the memory of the day wiggled, like a worm, back into my mind. I slowly rolled my head back and forth as I tried to ease the stiffness that had settled in my neck before I stood and walked out from beneath the tree.

The schoolyard felt strangely still, like the quiet that lies in the air right before a storm. I walked to the corner of the school as I searched for Denny since he'd said he would walk me home. Not finding him, I felt my heart start to race. I was certain something awful had happened to him because Denny would never forget me.

I quickly unhooked the rusty latch on the gray-speckled white school gate, cutting two of my fingers. Not wasting a minute, I put my fingers to my lips to stop the blood causing my mouth to fill with the taste of metal and dirt. I then tore down the dirt road that led home as fast as I could.

The smooth bottoms of my shoes caused me to slip once or twice, but I managed to steady myself even as I jumped over potholes. As I ran, I listened to my feet pound along Cooper Road as my head raced with the frightening thoughts of what happened to Denny.

I reached Higgins Hill, which sloped down past Widow McIntyre's house until it flattened again next to a large cornfield. Even though I was now close to home, I kept on running. I got going so fast down the hill that I felt like I could fly to the bottom until halfway down, my shoes slipped against the tiny stones causing me to ride the rest of the way down on my right side.

I screamed in pain until I finally slid to a stop. I lay there for a minute or two, trying to catch my breath. Carefully I lifted my head to look at my leg. Bits of gravel stuck to my scraped skin, which was oozing small streams of blood. I rolled onto my other side, and slowly stood up.

As I hopped to the side of the road, my leg began to sting causing my eyes to again fill with tears. Determined to keep going, I grabbed a large stick to lean on and started walking. Every step I took hurt, but I didn't stop because Denny wouldn't stop.

I hobbled to the corner of Farmer Eldridge's cow pasture where I was greeted by the stomps and stares of Black Angus. Even though I knew that I would soon be nearing the broken-down barn where Denny and I used to play, I had to rest my leg. I walked through the dried grass until I reached a stump with peeling bark and roots that crept along the ground.

I sat down facing the old red barn with doors that swing in the wind. The man who owned the barn died many years ago making it the perfect place for me to hide out when Mother was in one of her moods. Denny often came with me on those days.

The sweet memories made on those long summer days came to mind and with them so did Denny. Because my worry outweighed my pain, I stood and painfully made my way back to the road where I'd only walked a few feet before I heard the sound of twigs snapping and cornhusks crackling as feet trampled them. I didn't see anyone until I got closer to the path that cut away from Byler Road.

Cupping my hand over my eyes, I squinted to see it was Denny. I opened my mouth to shout to him, but the words got stuck in my throat when I saw he wasn't alone. A girl was beside him. I took a few steps closer to get a better look.

Even though I could only see the back of her, it was enough to make out that she had long yellow hair that curled down to her waist and wore a pink dress that swayed back and forth as she walked.

I watched them until the light from the setting sun seemed to swallow them both in the reds and oranges of evening causing them to disappear from my sight. Turning, I headed home. I wanted to feel happy that Denny was fine, but all I felt was sad that he'd forgotten me.

I was dog tired by the time I'd reached our porch and in no mood for Caul, who started before I even got to the first step. "You are in so much trouble." Too tired to fight, I said nothing. Caul rocked on the porch swing so hard the chains jumped on the hooks like grasshoppers as he chanted, "You're in trouble. You're in trouble." Still ignoring him, I looked down at my new school dress then fanned it out to see how much was ruined. The hem was torn, the side was ripped, and the back was splashed with mud.

Seeing the torn, dirty dress stuck to my bloody leg, Caul slammed his feet against the porch. His shoes skidded against the wood, stopping the swing, causing the chain to bounce. Smirking, he said, "You are really going to get it now."

Knowing he was right, I tried brushing off the tiny pieces of stone stuck in my torn skin. Then I ripped the ribbon that had come loose from my hair and shoved it into the pocket of my dress. I pushed a few pieces of hair, which were clinging to my cheeks, from my face and brushed the front of my dress before I stepped onto the porch.

I stumbled back a few steps to keep from being hit as Mother pushed the door out toward me. It slammed against the wooden frame when Mother let go causing Caul to jump and me to take a few more steps backward.

Towering over me, she growled, "Where have you been?" Seeing my tattered dress and straggly hair, she didn't wait for an answer. She said, "Well, it's clear you've been wallowing in the mud like a pig."

Caul threw his head back with laughter then chanted again, "You're in trouble. You're in trouble."

Quickly turning, Mother tightly grabbed Caul's arm, pulled him up, and said, "That's quite enough, Caul. Get inside. Now."

As the screen door slammed shut, Mother wheeled around to face me. Taking hold of both of my arms, she dug her fingers so deeply into my skin that I was sure she would pop the bones right out. Her hands shook as she held on to me, and her breath came out in hot bursts against my cheeks as she shouted, "How dare you? How dare you ruin this dress after I told you not to get it dirty." Pulling me roughly toward her, she nearly screamed as she said, "You ungrateful brat! I took in two weeks of sewing to pay for this dress, and you trash it like it's nothing. You will never have a store-bought dress again." Shaking me, she shouted, "Do you hear me? Never again."

Letting go of my arms, Mother pushed me back from her and said, "Do you hate me? Is that why you do these things? Is it?" Stepping closer, she yelled again, "Answer me!

Do you hate me?" I wanted to tell her that I didn't hate her, but that wasn't what came out when I opened my mouth.

Balling my fists by my sides, I shouted, "I do hate you!" With those words came the rest, jumbled and even louder as I screamed, "I hate you! I hate you!" My throat burned and my chest hurt, but I didn't stop even when Daddy scooped me into his arms.

I shut my eyes tight as he pushed me gently against his chest and whispered, "Shhh. It's all right. Shhh. Come on, now. You're all right." With his sweet words, my screams stopped. Wrapping my arms around his neck, I buried my head into his shoulder and sobbed.

Over my choked cries, I heard Daddy say to Mother, "I've got this. You go in the house." In the safety of Daddy's arms, I looked up to see Mother standing with her hands on her hips staring at me. Daddy tried again, "Go on in. We'll be in soon." Mother rolled her eyes, but this time she listened. Daddy put his cheek next to mine and said, "Come on. Let's go sit."

Leading me to the bottom porch step, Daddy sat next to me and asked gently, "What happened?"

I wiped my cheeks with the backs of my hands, sniffed a few times, and said quietly, "Nothing."

Sighing deeply, Daddy said, "It ain't right how you talked to your mother, and we'll be talkin' about that later, but right now I need to know what happened to make you do it." Tilting my chin toward him, he said, "And I ain't goin' to take 'nothing' for an answer."

I wanted to tell him about my fight with Caul, my ruined dress, and how Ms. Sprigg punished me for Billy poking me, but instead I took a deep breath and said, "Denny forgot me." As the tears again rolled down my cheeks, I added, "And I fell." I turned my leg to show him the cuts.

Pulling me toward him, he cradled me in his arms, trying to comfort me. I nestled into his neck and took in his sweet smell of coal dust, laundry soap, and pipe smoke. He gently rocked me side to side, smoothing down my hair as he listened to the rest of my story.

When I had finished, Daddy said softly, "Let's go take care of those cuts." He grabbed my hand and led me to the water pump at the front corner of our house. I sat down while Daddy gave the pump handle a hard push before quickly putting his handkerchief under the stream of water to soak it.

Kneeling next to me, he carefully dabbed the cuts. With the blood and gravel cleaned from my leg, Daddy pulled another clean cloth from his pocket, wrapped it around my leg, and said, "Now that this is taken care of, let's see if we can mend a bit of that pain in your heart."

Daddy leaned in close like he was going to tell me a secret and said, "Denny ain't a boy no more. He's becoming a young man who is startin' to like the company of young ladies." I sighed and turned my head. Daddy said, "Now, that don't mean he don't love you no more. It just means that his head is filled with other things right now making him a bit forgetful."

Daddy paused a minute and said, "I ain't sayin' what he did was right because part of being a man is keeping your word, but you will understand one day sooner than I'd like."

Suddenly mad again, I said, "No, I won't."

Daddy smiled and said, "You don't believe it now, but there will be a day when a young man is going turn your head, making you starry-eyed and forgetful." His smile slipped as he said, "When that happens, little girl, just make sure he loves you for you." As Daddy quickly turned his face from me, I thought I saw tears in his eyes, but maybe he was just tired.

I looked over at the edge of our yard to the big apple tree where Denny and I used to climb to the highest branch and spend our day cloud watching and talking. I wanted to believe what Daddy told me, but I couldn't imagine ever letting some boy or anything else come between Denny and me.

Daddy turned toward me again, cleared his throat, and said, "We need to talk about what happened with your mother before we go in." A bit sterner, he said, "Pretty dresses and fine dishware don't come easy. The truth is that mining don't bring much more than a sore back and lungs full of dust, so your mother does what she can to make us a better life."

Softening his voice once more, he said, "The Harlins has always been good people, but we was given some rough turns. Your mother just wants a smoother road for you children." I listened and nodded, but it seemed to me that Mother thought satin dresses and china plates would make folks forget we were Harlins. I think no matter how bright the ribbon, if folks think it's tied on trash then they just think it's a waste of good ribbon.

Daddy quietly groaned as he stood and said, "Well, let's finish washing up and get in for supper." We both walked to the water pump where Daddy picked up the soap and started washing his hands. Frowning, he said, "No matter the soap or the scrubbin', I can't seem to get this coal dust off." Looking at his hands, Daddy turned them slowly front to back and shook his head. I think Daddy knew that while Mother tried to make everyone forget who we were with fancy things, it was his hands that kept reminding them.

Seeing me staring, Daddy quickly wiped his hands and then grabbed mine in the towel. As he dried my hands, he said, "You have pretty hands just like your mother." I pulled my hands back and shoved them into my pockets. Daddy tilted his head, gave a small smile, and said, "Let's go in now."

When we stepped onto the porch, I stayed stuck to the first step, worried that Mother would still be angry. Daddy opened the screen door and said, "Come on, we face our fears with our head up." As I stepped inside the kitchen, the syrupy smell of apple dumplings drifted into my nose making my stomach ache with hunger. Seeing us, Mother set the food on the table.

Without a word to each other, we sat down, and reached our hands toward one another. Mother's fingers barely touched the tips of mine as she said grace. Finishing the prayer, she quickly pulled her hand away from mine letting me know that she'd not forgotten my ruined dress and she wasn't going to let me either.

Although Denny's seat was empty, Mother still piled fried chicken and buttered peas on a plate for him. Daddy said, "A little bird told me that Denny was out walking with a young lady late this afternoon." Daddy winked at me.

Mother scooped a big spoonful of mashed potatoes next to the chicken and said, "Was he with that Persimmon girl?" Daddy shrugged. Mother's eyes lit up as she said, "I hope it was her. She's from such a good family." Daddy shrugged again. Mother said, "You know them. They're the ones who live on Hyland Drive in that grand house with the big white pillars." Mother then described the sparkling picture windows with flower boxes and the rosebushes that clung to the side of the house like if she could picture it well enough then some part of her could be there too.

Daddy waved his hand in front of Mother, breaking her stare before he said, "The boy is only fifteen. Instead of planning his wedding, we should be more worried about him gettin' home in time for supper."

Mother waved her hand and said, "Dinner can be warmed."

Looking from me to Mother, Daddy said, "He also forgot to walk his sister home from school."

Spooning more potatoes onto Denny's plate, Mother said, "I didn't know of any such plans." Without looking at me, Mother said, "It seems to me that she should understand since she don't do what she says neither."

Daddy said, "She waited for him. It's the reason the girl was late and the reason—"

Mother cut in and said, "She shouldn't be leaning on Denny so much." Mother held the spoon, still sticky with mashed potatoes, in the air as she turned toward me and added, "She's too needy." Mother's final words quieted the kitchen as she stood clutching the piece of silverware as if it were a prize for another one of her wins.

When supper ended, Mother cleared the dirty dishes from the table as Daddy went into the other room to read his newspaper. Caul slunk away to his room but not before looking at me and sticking out his tongue. Left alone in the kitchen, Mother and I spent the next half an hour washing and drying dishes in silence.

Stacking the last dish into the cupboard, she said, "Go and change into your nightgown." As I turned to go, Mother said, "Leave your dress on my quilting rocker. I'll try to mend some of the holes." Sighing, she added, "Maybe you can get a few more wears out of it." It was the first kindness Mother had shown me since we'd fought on the porch. Grateful for it, I reached my arms out to hug her. She looked at me then turned back to the sink. I let my arms drop back to my sides and went to my room.

I slipped my head into my softest nightgown, careful to choose one that didn't brush too much against my sore leg. I then gently laid my torn dress across Mother's rocker before I headed down the hall. Hearing me, Daddy lowered his paper and nodded for me to come sit.

I curled myself next to him, and he wrapped his arm around me and pulled me close to him. I laid my head against his chest and listened to the steady beat of his heart. I tried to keep my eyes open but soon my eyelids felt heavy, and I was asleep.

"You're home a bit late, ain't ya?" Daddy's voice made a deep rumbling sound in his chest, waking me. I kept my eyes closed and listened.

"I know. I lost track of time," Denny said.

I could hear Daddy close his newspaper as he said, "You missed supper."

Denny said, "I'm sorry, I can tell Mother—"

Daddy cut in and said, "It's not all you missed."

Denny was quiet.

Daddy said, "You missed getting your sister from school."

I could hear Denny groan as he remembered then asked, "Is she mad?"

Daddy said, "Not mad but hurt. She looks up to you, you know. She depends on you." I could feel Daddy's arm tighten around me as he said, "I know it's a lot to put on a young boy, but it's good for her to have someone in her corner. She needs it." I heard the crinkle of his paper as he set it down before he said, "I understand how a pretty girl can turn a man's head in only one direction. Maybe it ain't right, but I'm askin' you to watch out for your sister."

Denny said, "I will, and I am sorry."

"Your mother fixed you a big plate. Go on in and eat somethin'," Daddy said.

I could hear Denny shuffle closer before he said, "If you don't mind, I'd like to carry her to bed and tuck her in."

Daddy laughed. "You sure you can carry her?"

Denny slid his arms under me and said, "Sure. She's just a little thing." I could feel Denny strain under my weight as he lifted me, but I still pretended to be asleep.

I heard the hinges creak as Denny opened my door. Pulling back the covers, he gently rolled me under them. Placing my favorite quilt beside me, he whispered, "I'm sorry I forgot you, Birddog. I promise I won't do it again."

Quietly he shut my door leaving me alone in my dark bedroom, where I listened to the familiar sound of squeaking floorboards and the murmur of voices. Wrapping my blankets tighter around me, I again felt warm and safe, and not forgotten.

CHAPTER
SIX

The following morning, I woke to the sun streaming through my bedroom shutters. I watched the casts of light dance across my floor as I tried to shake sleep from my body. I then got out of bed, went to my window, and pushed open one of the slates of the shutters. The tops of the trees were tipped in gold, showing the beginning colors of fall.

The wooden floor was cold on my bare feet, so I hurried to get dressed. I pulled a white cotton slip from my top drawer. As I slid it over my head, I remembered my ruined dress and worried about what I would wear. That's when I saw it. Lying on the small stool that sat in the corner of my room was the prettiest dress I'd ever seen.

I picked it up and held it beneath my chin. I walked across my room and peered into the mirror to see that it was my ruined dress mended and perfect. I then whirled it back and forth causing it to fan out and fold back around my legs, admiring the beautiful blue patches with white stitching. Before putting on the dress, I turned it over to see that the zipper had been replaced with small pearl buttons like the ones on Mother's favorite blue dress. As the soft material slipped over my shoulders and tumbled to my knees, I slid into my worn shoes. Putting my hand on the doorknob, I looked back at my reflection and smiled.

Stepping into the kitchen, I could smell last night's dinner, which still lingered in the air. Mother followed, fastening her hair back as she headed for the cupboard. Glancing at me before turning to the stove, she said, "I see you found your dress."

Happy, I said, "Yes. Thank you for mending it."

Over her shoulder, she said sharply, "You can thank me by not ruining this one. I was up most of the night repairing it." My smile slipped as I sat and quietly waited for breakfast.

Mother stomped noisily around the kitchen as she pulled ingredients from the cupboards. Over the loud sound of pans being banged against the cook stove and the sizzling of the skillet, I didn't hear Denny come in until he said, "Good morning, Mother."

I looked up to see him give Mother a quick kiss on the cheek as he stole a piece of bacon. Mother playfully swatted his arm then looking at me she said sternly, "Your brother is kind enough to walk you to school today so you need to eat quickly so he isn't late."

I nodded then hid behind my schoolbook. Sitting beside me, Denny asked, "Getting a head start, huh?" Then reaching over, he turned the book right side up and smiled. Mother scooped an egg onto my plate along with a piece of toast and said, "Hurry up!" I'd only taken two bites of the egg when Mother said, "Time to go."

I grabbed the piece of toast and followed Denny to the door. Stopping for a minute, I flattened my dress down with my hands and fixed the hair ribbon. Denny looked over at me and said, "You're as shiny and pretty as a new penny, Birddog." I shrugged, but secretly I was prouder than I'd ever been as I walked out the door behind him.

Stepping onto the porch I was surprised to find Mother beside me. Flushed, she leaned close to me and warned, "You be nice to her."

Before I could ask who, Denny said, "Hi, Posey. You're right on time."

Walking toward the porch with her long pale arms wrapped around her books and her hair pulled back in a big yellow bow, she said, "Good morning, Denny."

I looked over at my brother, who beamed as he raced down the steps to take her books. Then with a goofy grin, he looked back at Mother and me and said, "I want you to meet someone. Mother. Birddog. This is Posey Persimmon."

Mother nearly tripped trying to reach out her hand to Posey. Posey smiled and said, "Nice to meet you, Mrs. Harlin." Then she looked at me and said, "It's nice to meet you too, Birddoo."

Denny laughed harder than I thought he should before he said, "It's Birddog."

Posey sniffed and said, "Sorry, but it's a bit of an odd name for a girl."

Mother nodded in agreement and said, "It's not her given name, but it seems to have become so thanks to my son." Mother winked at Denny then nudged me toward the steps before she said, "Enjoy your walk." Then looking just at me, she said, "Don't be a bother."

Without another word to me, Posey grabbed Denny's arm and turned toward the road. I followed behind, watching her yellow dress swish back and forth. We'd only walked for about couple minutes before Denny turned around to me and said, like I'd won a prize at the fair, "Hey, Birddog. Ain't we luck to have the prettiest girl in town walk with us today?" Without waiting for an answer, Denny turned back to Posey, who giggled like she'd never been called pretty before.

Walking a few paces behind them, I could still hear Posey as she babbled on about her favorite dresses and her perfect dream home. Pushing her long hair back, she said, "I want to live in a house with no less than five bedrooms and there *has* to be a big porch."

Looking at Denny, she asked, "What about you? What kind of house do you want?"

Denny shrugged and said, "I dunno. I guess I never gave much thought to it."

Wide-eyed, Posey said, "What? How could you not think about where you want to live?"

Denny shrugged again and said, "I guess I just never had much need to think about it."

Posey stopped walking, put her hand on Denny's arm, and asked, "Don't you want better?" Denny gently shook off her arm and started walking again. Quickly catching up, she said, "I didn't mean it like that. I just mean...doesn't everyone want...more?"

Denny nodded and said, "Of course." I didn't say anything, but that's when I decided that Posey Persimmon wasn't any prize.

Turning the final corner onto Cooper Road, I was happy to finally see the schoolyard. I'd had more than my fill of hearing about fancy dresses and colored barrettes even though Denny listened closely as if there was nothing more interesting than hair bows. As I watched Denny leaning close to Posey, nodding and smiling, I wondered how my brother, who used to talk about his love of animals and his dreams about leaving this town, could suddenly find hair bows so fascinating.

Denny turned around and said, "This is your stop, Birddog." I nodded and started toward the school. Sounding surprised, Denny said, "Birddog?"

I looked back and mumbled, "Thanks for walking me to school."

Denny walked over to me and asked, "Are you all right?"

Seeing Posey staring at us, I said, "Yeah, I'm all right."

Denny looked uncertain but before he could say another word, Posey whined, "Come on, Denny. I don't want to be late."

Torn but only for a moment, Denny said, "I'll see you at home, Birddog," before running to catch up to Posey.

Watching them walk away with their arms linked, I heard Posey say, "Did you see what Sarah wore yesterday? She looked like she just threw on a gunny sack." Her laughter trailed behind her as they walked away. They were soon out of earshot, which didn't matter because I'd heard enough to know that Posey was only pretty on the outside. Before I turned I heard Caul behind me as he sneered, "Looks like you ain't Denny's favorite no more." Ignoring him, I headed toward school.

I hadn't taken more than four steps when I felt my legs being pelted by small pebbles. I turned around to see Caul with a handful of stones and a spiteful grin. "Stop it, Caul," I said. He pulled another rock from the pile and chucked it at me, hitting me on the arm. Taking a step toward him, I shouted, "Stop it right now!"

Caul picked up another stone and said, "Or what?"

Stepping even closer, I knocked the stones out of his hand and said, "I'll make you." As soon as his carefully collected pile fell to the ground, I knew I'd made a mistake.

Even though Caul was only two years older than me, he was bigger and meaner. He quickly grabbed my arm and twisted it behind my back, pulling up until I cried out in pain. "Say mercy," he taunted. Stubborn, I said nothing. He yanked hard on my arm, forcing me to call out mercy several times before he let go.

Pushing me from him he said, "You can't *make* me do anything." Rubbing my arm, I walked away. Caul caught up and said, "See you after school." Then he showed me his pockets filled with stones and said, "It's going to be a fun walk." Laughing, he ran past me.

CHAPTER
SEVEN

I slipped into class unnoticed, except by Billy, who quickly waved his hand back and forth trying to get my attention. Quietly I sat beside him and whispered, "What?"

He leaned in and whispered back, "I wanted to get a closer look to see if your nose was flat from standing against the board yesterday." As the corners of his mouth slowly turned up, I thought that if the devil rested anywhere, it had to be in Billy's smile.

Billy asked, "Did you get in trouble at home?" I shook my head and buried my face in my book. Billy got the hint and started drawing on his desk.

Peering over my book, I watched Beverly Cobberson and Virginia Anne whispering and giggling. I watched them as they whispered secrets to each other and sketched pictures on one another's notebook. I watched them be friends. Feeling me stare, Beverly turned and said, "What are you looking at, Fat Head?" I quickly looked back at my page.

I spent the rest of class with my head down, only looking up when I needed to copy Ms. Sprigg's lesson from the board or to watch the minute hand slowly tick around in a never-ending circle. Even though numbers and words filled my notebook pages, I thought of little more than how Denny could like a girl who was as interesting as wet newspaper.

Three o'clock and my freedom came with a thud as Billy shoved me out of my seat. As my backside hit the floor, he leaned over and said, "School's done, Peacock." Beverly looked down and laughed. Stepping over me, Virginia grabbed Beverly's arm and laughed with her. I slowly stood, gathered my books, and went outside to wait for the wrath of Caul.

I stood by the school gate until the last person lifted the latch and headed down Cooper Road toward home. I waited for a few more minutes, but Caul never showed. Even though I was grateful not to walk home with him, I was worried Mother would be mad at me if I didn't, so I looked for him in his classroom and on the playground. I finally found him beyond the schoolhouse with a handful of erasers. Caught in a cloud of chalk dust, he choked and sputtered, "If you tell Mother, I'll really get you." I nodded before I walked away, smiling that instead of getting mine, Caul was getting his.

Since Caul was clapping erasers, I didn't have to spend my walk home in a run, so I sat down on the soft grass and took off my shoes. Spreading my toes apart, I wiggled each one. Then I tied the laces of my shoes together, slung them over my shoulder, and started down the road.

Being a warm fall day, it felt good to have the cool road under my bare feet. I liked walking down Cooper Road because it was lined with emerald pines, flowing weeping willows, and big oak trees. Sometimes when the wind blew, I felt like I could hear the trees whispering about everyone who had walked down this road. I stopped for a minute and listened, wondering what they would say about me.

By the time I reached Higgins Hill, Widow McIntyre was gliding back and forth on her porch swing. Watching her, I tenderly touched the cut on my leg, which was still tender and raw. Looking back up at her, I thought about pain and how there seemed to be so many kinds. I waved. She didn't. She just kept on swinging and staring out at nothing.

Her long auburn hair tumbled down her shoulders, which were covered in a pretty blue wrap. A year ago, Widow McIntyre was young and pretty and her name was Elaina. Every day that I passed by her porch, though, she seemed to become a little more of a widow and a little less of Elaina.

I reached the bottom of the hill and walked over to the field where the cows were lazily grazing. I pulled out a few pieces of grass and stuck them through the fence trying to lure one closer to me. I so wanted to feel their soft fur on my fingertips, but each just stomped and stared. No amount of coaxing brought them closer. I angrily threw the grass at them, which only floated gently to the ground. I walked back onto the road certain cows wouldn't have made for good friends anyway.

Taking the turn onto Byler Road, I stopped and looked closely at the red barn on the corner. I hadn't been in the barn since Denny and I used to play together inside. Walking toward it, I saw the doors were shut tight instead of swinging wide open like usual. Still in my bare feet, I watched for pieces of glass as I carefully worked my way over rocks and broken slats to the door.

Lifting the board from the rusted latch, I could smell the damp rot of wood and see the spots where the paint had peeled. Putting both of my hands on the board, I bent my knees to give it one hard push when I heard the rustling of leaves underfoot. Startled, I dropped my arms, stood, and listened.

Peering down the road, I saw someone walking toward me. Knowing it had to be Denny, I smiled and started to run. I stopped short when I saw that the person was too tall with a walk too slow and uneven to be my brother. It wasn't until he was only a few feet from me that I saw it was Daddy.

With a loud squeal and feet that barely touched the ground, I crashed into him causing his hat and black metal lunch box to spill onto the ground. "Whoa there, little girl," he said before wrapping me in a tight hug.

Pulling back and seeing the mess I'd made, I said, "I'm sorry."

Smiling, he said, "Don't be. I wouldn't mind that kind of greetin' every day."

I picked up his lunch box and asked, "Why are you coming home so early?"

Daddy said, "Boss was nice today."

As we walked, Daddy fretfully rubbed his forehead. I watched, worried. Slipping my hand into his, I asked, "Why are you really coming early?"

He smiled at me and said, "No pulling the wool over you is there?"

I shook my head and waited for the real answer.

"Do you remember when I told your mother that I would take on some extra work?" I nodded. He continued, "Well, this work is in a different part of the mine. It's a little deeper down. When we was in the south tunnel the bird died."

I stopped walking and asked, "There are birds down there?"

Daddy said, "No. They don't live down there. We take a little one with us for safety. If there are dangerous gasses they affect the bird first because he's so small. The men then know they have to get out quick."

I gasped and let go of Daddy's hand. He said, "I know it sounds cruel, little girl, but the truth is that little bird saves a lot of men from dying." Daddy took my hand again as we started to walk.

We were both quiet the rest of the way until we reached the dirt road to our house. As we got closer we could see Mother hanging sheets on the clothesline. Daddy stopped and stared. Barely above a whisper, he said, "She looks like an angel dancing on clouds, doesn't she?"

He didn't wait for my answer, instead he stooped to pick some wildflowers that had inched their way along the edge of the road. He pulled a single daisy from the bunch and handing it to me, he said, "Let's just keep the story about the bird between us, okay?" He gently put his hand on my head, then letting my hair slip through his fingers he added, "I don't want her to worry." I nodded, even though I couldn't imagine Mother giving much thought to a dead bird.

As we headed toward the clothesline, Mother disappeared behind a sheet. I watched as Daddy put the flowers behind his back then peeked around the corner to surprise her. Startled, Mother jumped. Daddy laughed. Mother didn't. She snapped, "You scared me!" Snatching a sheet down from the line, she added, "It's not nice to sneak up on people."

Suddenly serious, Daddy said, "I'm sorry. I didn't mean to scare you."

Mother dropped her pins into the large pockets of her pin bag. As she tightened the bow and straightened her back, she said, "Well, you did." Looking at him a moment longer, she furrowed her brow and asked, "What are you doing home so early?"

Daddy smiled and said, "I came home early to see my beautiful wife." Handing her the flowers from behind his back, he said, "And to give her these." As Mother took the flowers, her cheeks flushed red. Daddy smiled until she said through clenched teeth, "You left work early? You left knowing that hours not worked are hours not paid?"

Daddy gently placed his hand on her arm and said quietly, "I'll be paid for the morning and most of the afternoon." Mother shook off Daddy's arm. Daddy said, "It's just one day."

Mother sniffed and said, "Yes, and it's only three children to feed." Turning sharply, she stomped toward the house.

Some of the flowers fell to the ground, leaving a trail of daisies and forget-me-nots. I looked at Daddy. His eyes were sad even as he smiled and said, "You go on. I'm goin' get cleaned up then I'll be in."

As Daddy headed to the pump, I started across the yard, picking up the dropped daisies along the way. I put them in my pocket to press later, so I could always remember what that little bird had given with his life and what my father had given with his love.

CHAPTER
EIGHT

The leaves had dropped from all the trees, leaving them bare and thin. The ground hardened with the cold and the sky darkened with winter's fading light. I stood on the bottom porch step, breathing in the fresh, crisp smell of coming snow and breathing out little warm puffs of white. The cold air burned my throat and lungs as I wrapped my brown coat, with the broken zipper, tighter around me. It was still and quiet except for Denny's and Daddy's laughter as they tried to string the bright colored lights from one end of the porch to the other.

"Birddog, are these straight?" Denny yelled to me while holding the string above his head and twisting his body around to keep it even with Daddy's end. I looked for a minute, then cocking my head to the side I said, "Now they are."

Laughing, Denny pulled up on his side until the bulbs bobbed evenly down the line. Then leaning over the railing he shouted to Daddy, "I'm not sure they will be straight once we hook 'em."

Daddy shouted back, "My cold hands say they're good enough. I'll turn 'em on and you get your mother and Caul."

Standing huddled in front of our porch, we quietly watched the soft lights dance against our dark house. Daddy told me that he'd bought the lights at Walden's Hardware for no more than a song and the change in his pocket. There weren't many bulbs on the string and most of them were scratched, but when lit that cheap string of lights looked like a hundred different colored fireflies clinging to our house.

Breaking the silence, Mother said, "You two did a wonderful job. The house looks so festive and inviting with all those pretty colors."

Daddy playfully bowed and said, "Thank you." Pointing to me, he added, "Birddog made sure we got it straight and even."

Mother nodded. Looking at me, she smiled and said, "These things often need a woman's good eye."

Daddy gently squeezed my shoulder as Caul muttered about being cold. Agreeing, everyone went into the house except for me. Standing alone on that cold winter's evening, I couldn't remember a time I'd ever felt warmer.

Christmas was only a week away, but to me it felt like it would never come. After dinner, I ran to my room, as I had done for the past week, to rip off one of the links from the red and green paper chain that Daddy had made for me to count down the days.

I tore the ends of the long piece of red paper apart and sat down on my bed to read the message he'd written inside. Smiling, I opened my nightstand drawer. I placed Daddy's silly poem on top of the others I'd saved then I took out the small box that lay next to them and closed the drawer.

Hearing a knock on the door, I quickly shoved the box under my pillow. Mother stood in my doorway holding something behind her back. Clearing her throat, she said, "I have something for you for your Christmas party tomorrow." Then she held out her arm to show me the most beautiful dress I'd ever seen. It was dark green velvet with a white lace collar and a wide sash that tied around the waist in a big bow.

Breaking my stare, Mother held it up to me and said, "Try it on." Once Mother slipped the dress over my head, she pulled at the edges to make sure of the fit. As I ran my hands up and down my sides to feel the soft and rough of the material, Mother said, "Turn around. I want to see if it needs altering."

Moving slowly around in a circle, I looked down at the puffy folds. Enjoying being wrapped in a cloud of green velvet, I moved my feet a bit faster. Soon I was spinning, wildly twirling my new dress around my knees in a swirl of Christmas color.

Grabbing me by the shoulders, Mother said sharply, "Stop that right now, young lady!" Dizzy, I swayed slightly as

LET THE WILLOWS WEEP

Mother said, "I made this dress so that my daughter didn't go to a school party looking like a ragamuffin." Straightening my sleeves, she snarled, "Not so you could spin around showing others your personals."

Embarrassed that Mother spoke about my underthings so openly, my face reddened as I mumbled, "Sorry."

Pursing her lips, Mother said, "I don't need 'sorry.' I need for you to behave. Understood?" I nodded. "Hang up the dress and don't wrinkle it." Mother warned. Then with one last look over her shoulder, she closed the door.

I was dressed before the sun had a chance to streak my room with the morning light. I pulled my hair back in a green ribbon to match my dress. Then trying not to wake anyone, I quietly tiptoed down the hall. Halfway to the kitchen, I remembered the small white box.

Turning, I walked back to my room, careful not to step on the boards that creaked under my step. I pulled the box out from underneath my pillow and carefully looked at it. The lid was a bit smashed and one of the corners was crushed from the night it spent under my head. Not caring I stuffed it into my bag.

By the time I reached the door, Denny had come into the kitchen. Yawning, he mumbled, "What are you doing up so early, Birddog?" With his eyes still swollen with sleep, he squinted to see the clock before he said, "You don't have to be at school for another hour."

Fidgeting, I rubbed my fingers, a nervous habit that I found comforting and Mother found irritating. Stammering, I said, "I'm, uh, I'm excited about the party. I want to…I want to get to school early." I couldn't tell him that the reason I was leaving early was because I couldn't listen to Posey's prattle for even one more day. Rubbing his eyes, Denny nodded then before turning to go back to bed, he said, "Have fun."

I smiled, grabbed my coat, and closed the door.

Stepping onto the porch, the icy air bit at my bare legs, stinging my skin. I wrapped my arms around my sides and braced myself for the long, cold walk to school. By the time I'd reached the schoolyard, my feet and nose were numb. Shivering, I opened the school doors and gratefully slipped inside the warmth.

The school was empty and quiet except for Mr. Ryers. The school janitor for twenty years, Mr. Ryers came early every day. He turned on the heat, opened the classrooms, and then when it was time he stood by the door and greeted us each with a smile. Caul said he was dimwitted. I thought he was kind.

I walked down the hallway to my classroom. Sliding down the wall, I sat next to the door and waited. Bored after only a few minutes, I pulled the white box from my bag. Opening it, I pulled a small pocketknife from its cotton bedding. Turning it over slowly in my hands, I studied the sawcut brown handle with the nickel silver ends. Carefully I pulled out the blade and laid it flat against my palm. Daddy told me it was a good gift for a boy. Maybe, I thought, but I wasn't so sure it was a good gift for Billy.

Hearing Mr. Ryers's footsteps, I put the pocketknife back into the box and shoved it into my bag. Stopping near my feet, Mr. Ryers said, "Hello, little miss."

I stood and said, "Hello, Mr. Ryers."

Smiling, he asked, "Why's you here so early today?"

Smiling back, I said, "Excited, I guess."

Mr. Ryers nodded then put his key into the lock, turned the knob, and opened the door. "Enjoy your party," he said before shuffling down the hall to open the other doors.

The empty classroom was still chilly so I kept on my coat as slid onto my seat. Ms. Sprigg came in first wearing a red sweater. The corners of her mouth were stained crimson from the lipstick she wore to match it and her hair was pulled tightly back showing the silver streaks that had settled into the other strands of brown. Putting her papers on her desk, she glanced at me. Her smile, pinched and forced, made me uncomfortable. I looked down and listened to the click of her heels as she walked up and down the aisles.

The long hand of the small clock on her desk clicked its way to eight. Within minutes, the classroom was filled with kids carrying handmade cards and paper-wrapped gifts. I looked at the other girls' dresses then down at my own.

Mine wasn't as fine as some, but it was prettier than most. Smoothing out the wrinkles and tightening the sash, I sat up a bit taller and called out to Beverly, "Merry Christmas."

Staring back, she looked at my dress, shook her head, and said, "Uh-huh," before turning back to Virginia.

Billy, who'd slid in beside me without my notice, leaned over and said, "Why do you bother with her? She's just mean." I looked at Billy, who smiled and said, "Green's a good color on you, Peacock."

I blushed and mumbled, "Thank you." And I meant it. Wrapping my fingers around the small white box, I was happy I'd listened to Daddy.

Ms. Sprigg lit the small Christmas tree on her desk then called everyone to attention. "Children. Children, settle down. We will begin our party with our gift exchange." Everyone in the class except for me erupted into giggles and squeals.

A week earlier, Ms. Sprigg had made us exchange names for gifts and my luck had it that I got Billy's name and he got mine. Now I was forced to give a present to the boy who spent most of his days poking me in the ribs and pushing me off of my seat.

Grinning, Billy brushed his hands over his olive-colored pants and said, "So, Peacock, give me my gift." Snickering, he nudged me and said, "Come on, mine first. Hand it over." Halfheartedly, I handed the little white box to him.

Taking off the lid, Billy looked inside. Wide-eyed, he stared for a minute before carefully pulling out the pocketknife. Smiling, he turned it over in his hands a few times before he quietly said, "Thank you." Then he slid a gift wrapped in red tissue toward me.

I gently slid my fingernail under the tape and peeled back the tissue. Tucked inside was a pretty tortoiseshell comb with tiny teeth. I looked up at Billy, who stammered, "My... my mother said girls like that stuff."

I nodded and said, "They do."

Billy lightly tugged my hair and said, "Now you can comb up all your feathers, Peacock."

Tucking the comb in my hand, I looked at Billy and said, "Thank you."

CHAPTER
NINE

Since I'd been walking home alone for weeks, I decided not to wait for Caul. Instead I ran most of the way only stopping now and then when my lungs burned too much from the cold. Reaching the porch steps, I barreled through the door and kicked off my shoes. Shifting my bag from one hand to the other, I pulled down the zipper of my coat then I yanked on my sleeves as I tried to get out of the hot, heavy layer of cotton wrapped tightly around me. Groaning, I tugged hard until my coat fell softly to the floor. Finally free, I raced to the kitchen, bursting to tell Denny about the Christmas party.

The sweet and steamy smell of baked goods filled the entire kitchen. Walking in, I could see Mother pulling a tray of gingerbread cookies from the oven. Denny breathed in and asked, "Did you make Grandma Anne's cookies?"

Mother smiled and said, "As I do every year." Mother slid the cookies onto a plate, which she placed in front of us. Looking at me, she said, "Go wash up properly and change out of that dress then you can help ice the cookies." Thrilled, I ran out without another word.

Coming back into the kitchen, I saw Caul with his finger stuck deep in the bowl. With Mother's head turned, he stuck a big blob of icing into his mouth before slinking off to sit in the corner. Calling me over to her, Mother slid a soft yellow apron over my head and tied it tightly in the back. "Ice the cookies, not your clothes." I smiled and happily nodded.

Putting little cinnamon button eyes on my cookie, Denny nudged me and asked, "Tell us about your party, Birddog."

I said, "It was fun."

Mother stopped stirring the batter. Encouraging me to say more she asked, "Was the room pretty?"

Putting down my cookie, I said, "It was so pretty. There was red and green streamers hung all over the room, and Ms. Sprigg had a little tree on her desk."

Mother seemed to stop listening as she started stirring the batter again, so I said, "My dress was the prettiest."

Placing the bowl to the side, Mother asked, "Really? It was even prettier than Mary Campbell's?"

Denny cut in, "Tell us what you got, Birddog?"

I shrugged and said, "Nothing too great."

Denny nudged me. "Come on. Show us."

I pulled Billy's present to me out of my bag and held out my hand.

Mother peered over the cookie sheet and said, "It's a beautiful comb and a very practical gift. You've needed a new comb."

Denny took a quick look and said, "Who gave it to you?"

I mumbled, "Billy Hawkins."

Denny laughed and said, "Isn't that the kid you socked in the eye last year?"

Without looking at Mother, I nodded.

Pretending she hadn't heard, Mother said, "I think it's quite a thoughtful gift for a young man to give."

I shoved the comb back into my bag and said, "It was his mother's idea."

Mother said, "Still, he agreed it was the right present to give."

Before I could argue, Denny said, "I think that Billy is sweet on you."

I snapped, "The only thing Billy is sweet on is food, most of which is smeared on his shirt and stuck between his teeth."

Denny tilted back his head and laughed. Mother turned to hide her own laughter, but I caught the few giggles that crept out like hiccups.

Pleased with myself, I decided to make them both laugh even harder. Standing, I began a full attack of Ms. Sprigg. "Billy is nothing. You should see my teacher. She looks like an old broom handle only her hair isn't as soft at the brush at the bottom." Just warming up, I added, "It would be okay if she was as useful as a broom, but she—" I stopped midsentence when I saw Mother's face redden with anger.

Pushing close to me, she said, "Where are your manners, young lady? Ms. Sprigg is a fine woman in the community and she deserves your respect." Turning away from me, Mother said, "Get to your room."

Denny shrugged and mouthed, "Sorry."

I grabbed my bag and walked out of the kitchen, leaving my gingerbread cookies unfinished and my heart broken. I shut my bedroom door behind me and sat on my bed. I could feel my throat tighten and my eyes sting as I tried to hold back the tears.

CHAPTER

TEN

I pulled my quilt around my shoulders and tucked it beneath my chin as I snuggled down into my warm bed. Rolling onto my side, I put my pillow over my head to cover my eyes from the sun that streaked across my floor and filled my room with light. I sighed, and closing my eyes I slipped back into a dream.

My name softly whispered in my ear brought me to the surface of sleep. Again Denny whispered, "Birddog." I groaned. Shaking me side to side, he said more loudly, "Birddog." I pulled the pillow tighter around my head. He laughed and shouted, "Birddog! Get up!"

Knowing Denny's doggedness, I pushed the pillow off of my head and said, "What?"

Denny answered, "It's goin' to snow today." I put the pillow back over my head, which Denny threw across the floor with my blankets as he said, "You can't sleep away the first day of Christmas vacation."

The possibility of snow stirred me, but I still wasn't in any hurry to get out of bed. Impatient, Denny said, "Come on, Birddog! I want to build a snowman bigger than last year." With a devilish grin, Denny said, "We'll have a snowball fight." Winking at me, he added, "It will be us against Caul."

Just the idea of socking Caul in the face with a snowball was enough for me to jump out of bed. I began folding the blankets and picking up my clothes as Denny headed toward the door. "Put on your warmest clothes. We're goin' be out all day," he called before closing the door behind him.

I hadn't spent the whole day with Denny in so long that my excitement had me running from my dresser to my closet as I tried to dress quickly. I couldn't believe that Denny, who had spent nearly every day of the last few months with Posey, was finally going to spend a day with me.

Opening my bottom drawer, I burrowed my hand down to the bottom as I looked for my longest scarf and thickest socks. Finding them, I put on the socks, tucked the scarf under my arm, and hurried out of my bedroom determined not to miss a moment.

We had finished breakfast when I looked out the window to see the entire ground covered in snow. Denny put his plate in the sink and said, "Hurry up, Birddog." I shoveled bits of egg into my mouth as Denny stood near the door tapping his foot.

Stuffing in the last bite, I pulled on my coat and waited with Denny as Caul slowed us down by peeling off more layers than he put on. "I'm hot," he muttered as Mother rewrapped the scarf around his neck and said, "I will not have a frostbitten child."

Mother took his piece of peanut butter toast and shoved his mitten onto his sticky hand. Caul licked the peanut butter from the corners of his mouth, smacking his lips together loudly as he followed Denny and me out the door.

I jumped off the bottom porch step and tilted my head all the way back. Soft snowflakes swirled around me silencing my world. I stuck out my tongue, allowing the tiny flakes to land and quickly melt in my mouth. Swallowing, it felt like winter was rolling down my throat deep into my belly. Slowly turning in circles, I watched as the snow blanketed the ground in white.

Kneeling into the cottony snow, I cupped my hands together scooping the snow into a small ball, which I carefully rolled until it grew into a much larger ball. "Denny! Help me build a snowman," I called as I continued rolling the snowman's head.

Running over to me, Denny said, "With all this snow, we can build a whole family." Crouching down next to me, Denny dug into the now deep snow as he began to make the body.

I'd just finished adding the snowman's eyes with Mother's old buttons when Caul ripped off the head and whipped it at Denny. Roaring with laughter, Caul ran as I yelled, "Get him, Denny!" Denny ran at Caul, hurling snowballs at him.

Smacking Caul on the cheek, Denny whooped, "Snowball fight!"

Staking our territory behind Daddy's woodshed, I tried to make snowballs as fast as Denny could throw them.

We were getting the best of Caul when Posey Persimmon strolled into our yard. Her yellow hair was brushed back and tucked under a large furry hat and her hands were hidden inside a matching white muff. Looking around, she called out, "Denny." Seeing her, Denny stopped chucking snowballs.

Taking off his glove, he quickly ran his fingers through his hair before brushing the snow off of his jacket. Then, without a word to me, he ran to Posey, leaving me alone with a pile of snowballs and a brother bent on revenge.

Peeking out from behind the woodshed to spy on them, I felt a hard chunk of snow thud against my ear and drip down my neck. Looking up, I saw Caul. With bits of snow still stuck to his gloves, he smirked and said, "You ain't so hard to hit without Denny to protect ya." I wiped the cold water off of my face with the back of my glove before I packed all the leftover snowballs into one giant one.

Hefting it up, I called out, "Hey, Caul!" Turning, he took the hit square in his big open mouth. With his eyes wide and watering, he sputtered and coughed as the ice slid uneasily down his throat.

I was already on the porch when he sputtered, "I'm goin' get you." Taking one last look at his pale wet face, I went inside, letting the door slam behind me.

CHAPTER
ELEVEN

I spent the late afternoon of Christmas Eve making everyone's presents. I took the most time with Daddy's gift, trying to make it perfect. When it was finally finished, I held it up by the string I tied through the hole in the top. I smiled at the perfection of the little bird I'd made with construction paper and glue. As I gently blew a small breath of air toward it, I watched the tiny wings flutter. I was happy that I could give Daddy a bird that didn't have to be caged—one that wouldn't die.

I gathered all the gifts into a small pile then slid them beneath my bed. Standing, I stretched my arms above my head before shaking loose the stiffness from my legs. Then squinting in the fading light of winter's fleeting afternoon, I opened my door and padded down the hall.

While my mother cleaned and my brothers played cards, I sat in Daddy's rocking chair listening to the soft creak of the rockers against the floorboards. The dim light of the candles bathed the room in a soft glow. Pulling my knees in toward my chest, I rocked back and forth as I watched the flickering of the tiny flames dancing like angels wrapped in wings of yellow and red.

"Is anyone home?" Daddy called out. "I have a delivery for the Harlin family." I slid from the rocker and hurried into the kitchen. Daddy stood in the doorway, smiling.

Caul pushed past me and asked, "What is it? Is it a bike?"

Mother pulled Caul back and scolded, "It ain't nice asking for what you know we can't afford." Caul slunk to the corner giving me room to get a closer look. Stepping inside, Daddy pulled behind him the biggest, greenest tree I'd ever seen.

Daddy dragged the tree into the front room, leaving a trail of pine needles behind him. Mother followed with her rusted metal dustpan scooping them up. In awe, we all watched as Daddy wrangled with the branches, which seemed to reach and poke into everything.

Pushing the tree into a corner, he smiled and said, "How's it look?"

Mother shook her head and said, "Big. Really big."

Smiling wider, Daddy said, "More room for your decorations."

Now Mother smiled.

Opening a box she'd taken from her room, Mother gently pulled out and unwrapped several glass angels and a few paper Santas. We each carefully hung them on the branches. Then after dinner, Daddy lit the tree. Together, we sat in silence surrounded by the warmth of the soft lights and the spirit of Christmas.

On Christmas morning the tree was brightly lit, but I hardly noticed with all the presents spilling out from underneath it. In truth, there really weren't that many gifts. A miner's pay doesn't bring much, but seeing a few boxes wrapped in red and green ribbon as Mother and Daddy stood smiling made me feel as though the floor was covered in gifts. Nudging us forward, Daddy said, "Go on. They ain't goin' open themselves."

We each ran to our spot under the tree and picked up the present with our name. With three gifts each, I took my time opening mine. Although newspapers were used for wrapping, the ribbon made them pretty. As I opened my final present, Mother said, "I think Santa may have been too generous this year."

Daddy smiled and said, "I think the kids might've been too good this year."

Carefully putting my opened presents under the tree, I gave my family the gifts I'd made for them. Caul opened his first, snorted, and threw it aside. Seeing Daddy glare at him, he mumbled, "Thanks."

Denny opened his next and said, "This is great. Thanks, Birddog."

As Denny put my gift to him with the others, Mother pulled loose the ribbon as she let the paper slip to the floor. I held my breath as she pulled out the small white handkerchief with her initials stitched crookedly at the top. Holding it up, she said, "It's quite nice." I smiled. Mother ran her fingers over the bumpy threads that crisscrossed unevenly and said, "And your stitching will get better with time and practice."

Daddy cleared his throat and said, "It's my turn." He gently turned the gift over in his hands. Praising me, he said, "It's wrapped so beautifully."

I smiled again and said, "Open it."

Daddy lifted out the tiny bird with a body made from paper and wings made of real feathers pulled from my pillow and said nothing. Instead he made it fly by blowing a soft breath of air toward it just as I had done.

Taking notice of us watching him, he cupped the paper bird in his hands and said, "It's…" Clearing his throat once more, he said quietly, "It's perfect." It was then that I wished I had a box big enough and strong enough to fill with this moment, so I could keep it forever.

CHAPTER

TWELVE

January spilled into our lives bringing a new year but much remained the same. Denny spent his days with Posey while Caul spent his trying to get even for the snowball he took to his face. My days were filled with long school hours and steering clear of Caul. The only change was that Daddy seemed to work harder and Mother seemed to notice him less.

Tiny sprigs of grass poked through the remaining crusts of ice reminding us that spring would come again. The hard coldness of the ground, however, wouldn't let us forget that winter wasn't over, and it wore at each of us. For me, it was the long, lonely walks home, cold to my bones from the bitter winds that chilled me.

Wrapping my coat tighter around me, I hurried home to the warmth of the cook stove and Daddy's lap. Tramping the snow and mud from my shoes, I walked into the kitchen to find Mother sitting at the table peeling potatoes. Without looking up, she asked, "Did you wipe your feet?" I nodded as I took off my coat. Mother stood and said, "Wash up then start peeling."

Walking to the stove, she stirred a large pot and asked, "Do you have homework?"

Working my way around a large potato, I said, "No." Mother cleared her throat and said, "No, ma'am." I repeated her words as I threw the peeled potato into a bowl. Taking the bowl, now filled, to Mother, I asked, "When is Daddy getting home?"

She sighed and said, "He will be home when he gets home."

I went to my room to wait.

For the last few weeks, Daddy and I sat together in the evenings. Him with his newspaper and me with my schoolbooks. Tonight was the same. Curled up in Daddy's lap, I listened to the soft crinkling of the newspaper pages while I carefully studied his face, which had more creases than a rumpled bedsheet. I'd noticed lately that Daddy started to wear tiredness like a second skin glued on too tight.

As Daddy turned the page, I asked, "How come you suddenly have so many wrinkles?"

Daddy sighed and said, "They ain't come on so quick. They've been hiding underneath for some time."

With my finger, I traced a wrinkle that ran like a deep ravine from the corner of his eye to the corner of his mouth then asked, "Why do some folks have so many and some folks don't?"

Daddy put down his paper and thought for a moment before he said, "I think that it depends on the kind of living you do." Daddy sighed and said, "A hard life brings on more wrinkles, and sooner."

Lowering my head, I mumbled, "I'm sorry."

Daddy squeezed me and said, "Ain't no reason to be sorry. I also have a lot of wrinkles from laughing." He smiled and so did I. We sat quietly enjoying the stillness that surrounded us until Mother appeared in the doorway.

With her hands on her hips, she shook her head and said, "She is getting far too old to sit on your lap."

Daddy pulled me closer and said, "She was just gettin' warm and telling me about her day."

Mother dropped her arms and said, "Fine. Five more minutes then bed." As the sound of Mother's footsteps faded down the hall so did Daddy's smile.

Gently taking my hand in his, he turned it from front to back and said, "Do you remember when I told you that your hands were like your mother's?"

Pulling my hand from his, I sighed and said, "Yes."

Daddy turned to me and said, "I know you don't like that they're the same, but it's true. What you need to know though, little girl, is what you do with them is your choice." I looked at my hands.

Daddy leaned back and rested his head for a moment before he leaned forward again and said, "We all make our own cages in this life, sweet girl. We build little metal bars from some decision or another until we're sittin' confused and trapped inside not knowin' how we got in." Daddy sighed and said, "Or knowin' how we can get out."

Taking my hand once more, Daddy said, "The harder your heart, the harder those bars are to break." Daddy wiggled my fingers and said, "You can use these hands to make little metal bars or you can use them to free others from their cages."

I nodded.

Wrapping his arms around me, he whispered, "I'm proud of you. You know who you are and you ain't willin' to change it for no one. Remember, little girl, paper birds ain't the only creatures that can fly free."

I pulled back and looked at Daddy's face. His eyes were as blue and full as the oceans on Ms. Sprigg's maps. Resting my head against his chest, I listened to the steady beat of his heart as he softly rocked us back and forth until we again became quietly lost in our own thoughts.

CHAPTER

THIRTEEN

I don't remember dreaming when I slept that night, but I do recall the nightmare when I woke. I sat straight up in bed with my eyes still half closed. My heart pounded inside of my chest so fast and loud, it was hard to hear Denny as he whispered, "It's okay, Birddog. It's Denny. I'm sorry I scared you." My heart didn't slow a beat. I guess my body knew what happened before my brain.

Sounding strained, he said, "There was a bad cave-in a couple of hours ago. The foreman called the fire company. They've been tryin' ever since…"

Confused, I rubbed my eyes and asked, "What happened?"

Denny shook his head and said, "There was an explosion, I guess."

Panicked, I shrieked, "Denny, what happened?"

Startled, Denny stuttered, "I…I don't know. I guess the tunnel collapsed."

Leaping from my bed, I nearly screamed, "Where's Daddy?"

Denny wiped the tears from his cheek and said, "I dunno. They're looking, but it's bad. Really bad." Denny tried to hold on to me, but his grief made him weak.

I ran into the kitchen where Mother sat alone at the table staring blankly at the door as if she believed he would just walk in, and it would all be over. Never breaking her trance, she looked right through me as I swung open the door, letting it slam behind me. Running down the road toward the mines, I was determined to save Daddy. I would dig him out with my bare hands. I wouldn't let him lie in the ground, cold and alone.

By the time I'd reached the end of our road, the sky was lit in a pink haze of morning light. The wind, which stung my cheeks and burned my eyes, also caught my breath starting a fire in my lungs. My body begged to stop, but my heart wouldn't allow it. Seeing Daddy before my every step, I ran faster toward the dark hole where he waited.

Racing up Higgins Hill, my legs gave out causing me to fall onto the ground in a useless heap. I lay there hoping I was dying even as each puff of white breath that circled my face denied me that wish.

Shivering, I wrapped my arms around myself. Darting my eyes from side to side, I tried to figure out what was whimpering when I felt arms reach beneath me, scooping me up. As Mr. Eldridge held me close to him trying to soothe me, I realized the sound was coming from me.

Wrapped in his strong arms brought the missing of Daddy closer causing me to kick as I screamed, "Let me down! Let me down!"

My head pounded with the sound of my own fear and grief as Mr. Eldridge whispered, "Shhh, child. It's okay. Be still, now."

Unable to fight, I lay my head against his chest and sobbed until my choked cries became soft hiccups. Taking a deep breath, I could faintly smell manure and aftershave, scents that had permanently pressed themselves into Mr. Eldridge's shirts after so many years of farming. Exhausted, I sunk deeper into his arms and closed my eyes.

I knew Mr. Eldridge as the farmer at the bottom of Higgins Hill since I was little but as his strong arms sheltered me from the cold and my sadness, I also came to know him as kind. Tucking the flaps of his plaid coat around me as he carried me down Byler Road toward my house, I buried my head into his neck and cried because I'd left Daddy in some dark hole, and I cried because Daddy left me.

FOURTEEN

I could feel a tightening around my neck choking me. Grabbing at my throat, I pulled back the stiff sheet that tangled around me. Shoving the covers off of me, I felt them pulled back over me as he said, "You are going to be okay, but you need to keep covered."

I didn't want to disobey Daddy, but I could feel the heat from layers of cotton quilts on every inch of me until I thought I would melt. Again, kicking the blankets off of me, I turned to look at him, but my eyes, heavy with sleep, closed.

Slipping into the darkness behind my eyes, I saw the cold, hard ground before me. Sinking my fingers into thick layers of rock and dirt, I pulled away stones and scooped out handfuls of gravel as I dug deeper and deeper into the Earth looking for the little bird buried beneath. I pulled back my cut and blackened hands, then as I plunged them back into the sharp stones I heard voices all around me. Unable to shout out, I was forced to listen.

"I don't understand why we have to wait this long. They should have uncovered him by now." The familiar voice rose in anger. "They can't expect us to sit and wait, holding on to some shred of hope that he survived just so they can come and take it from us. I will not suffer his death twice. I want him out. Now!"

My eyes fluttered but unable to open them, I still knew it was Denny's voice when he said, "I know it's hard, Mother. We have to let them do their job, so we can focus on Birddog." Lowering his voice, he added, "She's so sick."

"I don't understand why that child must make everything so much worse. Why in the name of God would she run outside half-naked in the dead of winter?"

Confused, I listened as Denny said, "She was in shock, Mother."

I could hear the anger in Mother's voice rise and crack into sobs as she said, "All she ever causes is trouble and heartache."

Slowly able to open my eyes, I could see Mother standing near my bed with Denny close beside her as Caul hid in the doorway. As my eyesight cleared, I could also see pain in their eyes. The same pain I felt in my chest when I remembered it wasn't a bird that was buried. It was Daddy.

My memory unearthed the grief buried in my heart causing the pain to sweep across my body until it came swiftly out of my throat in a scream that pierced the room's silence. I could feel hands and arms stretched across me like ropes of flesh keeping me down, yet I screamed.

"We have to calm her! Denny, please hold her leg more firmly. Mrs. Harlin, you must comfort her. She seems near hysteria," Dr. Miller said.

I knew Dr. Miller well. He'd been to our house many times as he tried to get me to swallow a bitter medicine for some cough or cold, and now here he was again trying to get me to swallow my grief.

Mother didn't take one step toward me. She didn't speak one word of kindness to me. In that moment, the pain of losing my father was doubled by the loss of my mother. I stopped screaming. Unsure of my sudden steadiness, hands were slowly and carefully lifted from my body. The room fell silent, but the sound of our grief was deafening.

The following day my fever broke, robbing me of the sweet dreams made in the stupor of my sickness. As the illness drained from me, my body returned to the world of the living, forcing my mind to accept that my father could be dead.

Pulling my quilt close to my cheek, I whispered into the soft cotton, "Daddy's gone." The words felt strange on my lips and sounded even stranger in my ears. I tried again, "Daddy's gone." I said the words over and over, again and again, as I tried to accept it, but I couldn't accept that the one person who loved and believed in me most could truly be gone.

Clasping my hands together tightly, I prayed, "Please God, don't let him be dead." I bit my teeth into my lip as I covered my mouth with my hand fighting the urge to scream.

Hearing three hard raps on my door, I looked up to see Dr. Miller with my mother and Denny following close behind. Stepping close to my bed, he took my hand, laid his fingers across my wrist, and asked, "How are we feeling today, young lady?" Before I could answer, he placed my hand back on the bed, turned to my mother, and said, "Her pulse is strong."

Pulling a small bottle from his bag, Dr. Miller said, "If she becomes…" He peered into his bag again as if looking for the word and said, "Restless." Handing the bottle to Mother, he said, "You are to give her only one pill." Picking up his bag, he added, "And she needs to stay in bed for at least another day or two to regain her strength." Mother nodded as she and Denny followed Dr. Miller out the door.

As my door was softly shut, I buried my head into my pillow. I closed my eyes escaping to the only place that brought me peace. The darkness behind my eyelids filled with the color of Daddy's blue eyes and the dim glow of the oil lamp. I gently rocked back and forth listening to the soft creak of Daddy's rocker in my mind. I wrapped my arms around my sides pretending they were Daddy's arms as he held me close. My throat tightened and eyes filled with tears as even my sweetest memories became too painful.

I didn't know how long I'd slept but when I opened my eyes, the pink and orange hues of early evening filled my room. I lay staring at the wall until the soft colors faded into darkness. I didn't get out of bed. I didn't turn on a light. Instead, I stayed in the dark wanting to become a part of it.

The house had been quiet for hours, so the loud knocking startled me. I jumped out of bed leaving behind my sadness and fear. Taking only hope, I ran to the kitchen. The steady banging brought each of us to the door like moths to a flame with no understanding that their curiosity would cause them to be cruelly devoured.

We drew close together, bumping into one another just as we had done the night Daddy brought home the Christmas tree only there were no smiles, no pushing, no racing. Instead, we took each step painfully slow as though trying to stop time in a moment that was safe before we opened the door and had every moment after forever changed.

Mother straightened her dress and pressed down the wrinkles. She then pushed back a few loose hairs before she reached for the knob. Keeping us tucked behind her, she took a deep breath and opened the door. A short thin man not much bigger than Caul stood on our porch. His face was small with beady eyes and a long nose that twitched in the night air. He looked more like a mouse than a man.

He licked his pale lips and said, "Evenin', ma'am." Mother nodded. Rocking from one foot to the other, he said, "I regret to inform you that your husband's body was found."

Mother said nothing.

Believing he hadn't been clear, he said, "Your husband is dead."

Mother leaned heavily into Denny.

Waiting no more than a few seconds, the mouse man's eyes widened as he excitedly told us the details of the explosion. Then, trying to hide his smile, he said proudly, "I was a big part of the rescue."

Mother stiffened. Pulling from Denny, she leaned close to the mouse man and screamed, "Rescue! *You* didn't rescue anyone." Pushing her nose almost to his, she hissed, "Don't talk to me about a rescue when my husband is dead!"

The mouse man dropped his head. Staring at his feet, he said, "We are all saddened by this terrible tragedy, Mrs. Hammond. As you can—"

"Harlin."

"Excuse me?"

"My name is Harlin and my husband's name is Harlin," my mother said. Her voice was steady but tears streaked her cheeks. She quickly wiped them away before she put her hand on the doorknob and asked, "Is there anything else?"

The mouse man stammered, "Uh…no. I guess not."

Taking a small cloth bundle from his pocket, he said, "Well, there's this." Handing it to Mother, he added, "These are his personal belongings."

Mother gently cradled the bundle in her hands. Before shutting the door, she asked, "How *did* you find him?"

Mouse man said, "It was his headlamp. All the other men's lamps had burnt out but not your husband's. His light burned bright enough for us to find them. It's strange, really. Those lights ain't supposed to burn that long."

Mother closed the door on his final words and as the latch snapped shut, I felt grateful that even in our darkest hour, Daddy had given us a bit of light.

CHAPTER

FIFTEEN

Studying myself in the mirror, my red-rimmed eyes inspected everything from top to bottom. I didn't have a black dress, so I had to wear my dark blue one with the loosened hem and the stain on the collar. It was the first time that the proper clothes seemed important to me, and today I felt ashamed that I didn't have them. I turned from the mirror, wishing that I could disappear as quickly as my reflection.

Today was Daddy's funeral, and there were so many small moments that would be forever attached to my mind while other details slipped away before they ever had a chance to make any mark. Memory is strange and sometimes cruel. The brain chooses what is kept and what is discarded without any regard to what the heart may want to keep. I clearly remembered Mother's upswept hair and Denny's sad eyes, but I couldn't remember how we got to the cemetery.

Standing on the hard, uneven ground in front of Daddy's grave, it seemed odd to me that so many people spent time digging Daddy out of the ground only so that we would have to pay to put him back down in it. Feeling the warmth of the sun on my cheeks, I squinted in the bright light as I looked to see remaining clumps of snow sparkling like crystals. I felt angry that the sun was comforting the world when ours was crumbling.

We stood near to each other as the preacher read Bible verses that had nothing to do with Daddy. Denny stood closest to Mother, watching her as though he feared she would disappear. Looking into her empty eyes and seeing her vacant stare, I knew that in many ways Mother was already gone.

Denny whispered, "Are you all right, Mother?" She didn't answer. Dropping her hand from Denny's arm, she took several steps back from the coffin. Denny tried to move back with her, but still blankly staring she slowly shook her head.

Grief had the ability to change a person entirely. I saw this in Mother. To me, she always seemed fierce and bigger than any worldly force, yet grief made her small. Oddly enough, grief made Denny seem larger. He was no longer a gangly boy with mussed hair and wild eyes. He now appeared to be sturdier somehow. His hair was neatly combed and his eyes had darkened. Grief had made Denny a man.

The preacher called to Mother, "Mrs. Harlin, will you please come forward."

Denny quickly offered his arm. Leaning on him, she walked toward the coffin until she again stood with us. Reaching down, the preacher scooped up some dirt and placed it in Mother's cupped hands.

Dutifully, she sprinkled the soft soil onto the coffin as the preacher said, "This man born of the earth is now returned to the earth in God's name." Following my mother, each of my brothers took a handful of dirt. I too placed dirt on Daddy's coffin along with the daisy I had pressed in a book so many months ago.

As my flower softly landed, the service over. Mother stood with her arms crossed over her breast looking much like she did when she'd stand in the doorway to call us to supper. Daddy always thought she was most pretty then. Looking at her now with her beauty swallowed by her sorrow she looked broken, and Denny with his arms around her for support looked much too young to lean upon.

Silently, we started across the cemetery. Mother and Denny first followed by Caul and me. Always teased or tripped, it was habit that made me turn to check on Caul, but looking at him I saw in his sad eyes that grief had chased all the wildness away. I also saw behind me Daddy's grave. I stopped and stood for a moment.

Watching the men bury him in shovelfuls of dirt, I mourned that Daddy, who spent most of his life underground, was forced there in death as well. I was grateful that Mother had at least chosen a plot near the clearing so the sun could shine on him.

As we weaved our way between the smooth stones standing at attention, Mother ran her finger across the top of a tombstone and said, "We can't afford no more than small headstone for your daddy. It will have only his name and the dates of his birth and death etched on it."

Denny gently put his hand on Mother's shoulder and said, "It's enough, Mother."

It wasn't enough. My daddy's life was so much more than a dash between dates. I said nothing, though, because I knew that even with money there wouldn't be enough stone for all the words I wanted to say.

Nearing the road, I lagged behind watching my family that was now smaller, broken. I couldn't help staring at Mother and Denny. Wobbling like a child learning to walk she leaned into him, and like a protective parent he held on tightly to save her from the fall.

As the sun cast across Denny, I saw that his hair, like Daddy's, was black as pitch. I wondered if this made Mother sad, but as I watched her brush back his hair, I remembered that Denny had a light around him that would forever shine in Mother's eyes. In that moment, I wished for more than anything to have just a bit of that light.

SIXTEEN

Mother slowly opened the door and we stepped inside of a house that felt a little less like home. Quickly taking off her gloves, Mother went into the front room as we followed behind. Ripping her prized ornaments off of the tree, she grumbled, "He said he would take this tree out a week ago."

Denny swiftly grabbed hold of the glass angels before they crashed to the ground. Placing them carefully in the box, he said, "It's okay, Mother."

Mother snapped, "No, it's not. He *said* he would take it down, and now we have people coming to the house."

Again trying to calm her, Denny said, "They ain't goin' care about a tree. That ain't why they're comin'."

Paper Santas scattered across the floor as Mother dropped them and said, "I know why they're coming, and *I* care about the tree." As Mother jammed her fingers back into the branches, we heard a knock.

The Bailey family was first, then the McConnells, then the Cahill family, and then it was a steady stream of faceless mourners bringing their covered dishes and their pity. Miners most of them. They were kind, but I could see the fear in their eyes and the gratitude that they weren't us. I was sad that I wasn't one of them. They, with their unbroken family, would go to a house that was still a home able to face their tomorrow because their today wasn't destroyed.

Their hands stained from soot and their faces red from scrubbing, the men inched forward into our house at their wives' prodding. Some of the wives arranged casseroles and wiped a clean table while others fluttered around Mother whispering words that were meaningless to her.

I stood alone by Daddy's rocker watching people as they milled around talking about the weather and the rising price of vegetables. Some came close to me wearing a sad smile as they nodded their sympathy. My brothers shifted with almost motionless movements among these groups. The men squeezed their shoulders and shook their hands, welcoming them into a world where they were still too young to belong.

The afternoon silently slipped into evening. Dusk settled over our house, darkening our now empty kitchen. Mother sunk heavily into the chair Denny pulled out for her. He then brought her a cup of tea, which she never touched. Denny asked, "Do you need anything, Mother?" Mother shook then dropped her head.

Staring at her hands as she roughly pulled and rubbed her fingers, she said, "His hands were always stained." Mother was quiet for a minute then sighing, she said, "I knew it was dangerous, but I never said he had to work there." Her voice grew louder as she said, "Sure we needed things, but there were other jobs. He could have..." Mother didn't finish her sentence, instead she buried her face into her hands.

Kneeling in front of Mother, Denny gently took her hands in his and said quietly, "It's all right. We are going to be all right."

Like a child, Mother wailed, "How?"

Denny said, "I talked with Willard Bailey. He said they're looking to hire some men."

Mother gasped and shrieked, "No! You will not go down there."

Denny said firmly, "I will do what I have to for us to survive, Mother."

Mother grabbed Denny's shoulders and said, "You are not a man. You are a boy. My boy, and I won't lose you." Shaking his shoulders, Mother begged, "Please, Denny. Promise me!"

Denny swept Mother into his arms and without making any promises said, "It's all right, Mother. It's all right." Seeing the determination in my brother's eyes as my mother, defeated, slumped against him, I knew it would never be all right again.

As I watched Denny comfort Mother knowing what he planned to do, I panicked. I ran into the front room and slid into Daddy's rocking chair. Wrapping my arms tightly around me, I saw it tucked beneath red tissue paper. Slipping off of the rocker, I picked up the paper bird with crayon colored eyes.

As I held it up, watching it softly sway back and forth, I was angry that God took Daddy as easily as he took a bird with no more notice to one than the other. I was angry that Daddy left me and I was angry that Denny threatened to do the same.

I grabbed the fragile paper body in my hands and began to tear at it, watching as the small pieces fluttered to the floor. I ripped some of the feathers from the wings before Denny shouted, "Birddog! What are you doing?" Without waiting for an answer, he dropped to the floor to gather the shredded bits.

Showing me the torn pieces in his hands, he said, "This was his gift. You had no right to ruin it." Denny picked up a few feathers then realizing the hopelessness of piecing it back together, he stopped. With tears in his eyes, he said, "He loved it."

Still holding the carcass of my paper bird, I sunk to the floor and cried, "I know." Denny slid next to me and wrapped his arm around me as he leaned his head into mine.

As we sat silently we knew there was nothing more to say because sometimes life is just like paper wings. Fragile, easily torn apart, and often there are too many pieces to pick up.

CHAPTER
SEVENTEEN

Days were hollowed out by hours, which collected together in minutes of dreary details and the exhausting effort to keep going. Our father was dead, our mother sat idle, and we stayed quiet. I guess we each were waiting for a moment when our life would begin again.

For us, time had stopped. The life within these walls was nothing more than snaps of pictures twisted and trapped in a moment that refused to move forward. Sitting in Daddy's rocker, I looked around. The memory of him flooded into every space, seeping into the walls and floors until the entire house felt like an uneasy ghost. Everything that was once familiar and comfortable became haunting, holding us tightly to our grief.

The effort to move forward felt unbearable, but Denny never stopped trying. Stepping close to the Christmas tree, he began to take down the remaining ornaments. As he slipped a paper Santa from the broken bough, needles sprinkled around his feet. Mother, who sat silently staring, paid no mind to the mess.

Slowly rocking, I watched Denny as he carefully collected the ornaments and placed them back into their box. The brown bowed limbs of the tree lay limp causing two forgotten angels to dance upon the bent branches. Seeing three more ornaments lie scattered on the floor and the shadows of shattered people step beside them, I was suddenly very tired.

I lay my head back, closed my eyes, and listened to the soft tapping sound of my head against the wooden back. Denny's voice pulled me sharply from my sleep and the peaceful dream that released me from waking hours too heavy with hurt. "Birddog!" Denny said.

I opened my eyes. Denny stood in front of me holding a small box in his hands. With his eyes filled with tears, he looked at me and said, "It's for you. It's from…"

Daddy's name, which once slid off of our tongues so easily now often caught in our throats.

Taking the small box in my hands, I asked, "Are you sure it's for me?" Denny nodded. The box was so small it fit in my palm, but the mystery of it held a power that caused even Mother to turn toward it.

I looked at Denny who said, "Go ahead. Open it." I slowly lifted the lid. Inside lay a small oval brooch with lilac colored beads.

Peering from across the room, Mother said, "What is it?" I tilted the box to show her. Seeing the pin, she was quickly on her feet and at my side. Snatching my gift from my hand, her fingers skillfully turned it over and back again. She said, "I thought this was lost years ago."

Coming over for a closer look, Denny asked, "What is it?"

As Mother's lips slipped into a thin line, she said, "Not what but whose." She said, "It was your grandmother Harlin's brooch. She wore it every day or at least all the days I knew her. She gave it to your daddy on account she didn't have any daughters." Mother closed her fingers over the pin. Clenching her hand into a fist, she said, "I always thought he would give it to me."

Towering over me, Mother seemed taller than a tree and fiercer than the wind that bends it. She released her grasp, and the pin hit the floor, bounced once, and landed near my foot with a soft thud. I slid my hand to my foot, tightened my fingers around the pin, and pulled it close to my chest. Mother took a step back, but I didn't loosen my grip. Looking at Mother I knew I hadn't won. Instead, we silently struck a deal. She allowed me to have the last precious piece of Daddy, but in doing so, she would refuse me any part of her.

Mother raged like a storm as she stomped from room to room in gusts of thunderous movements. She pulled clothes from dresser drawers and coats from closets. After frantically searching the pockets, she dropped pants and shirts onto the floor. Tramping over the piles of clothes, she stormed into the kitchen where she flung open cupboards before attacking the drawers of the sideboard.

Denny trailed after Mother barely escaping slammed doors. I hid in the hallway, listening to Denny as he pleaded, "Mother, please stop." Mother's madness only swelled, spreading throughout the entire house until everything we owned was heaped onto the floor.

Her fury was fleeting, though, and soon she gave up her search. Sliding down the wall, she slumped over and cradled her head in her hands. Denny and I watched as Mother turned from a woman wild with determination to a crushed child.

Gingerly, Denny touched Mother's shoulder, but she didn't look up. Turning to me, he whispered, "Help me grab some of these things and put them on the table. We'll sort out everything later."

My hand barely grazed the edge of a coat when Mother lifted her head. Looking past Denny, she laid her eyes on me with the force of a hand and said, "Leave it! Leave it all." I dropped the coat as she dropped her head.

CHAPTER
EIGHTEEN

The weeks wore on, and soon we were forced to fit ourselves back into a life that now seemed small and unimportant. School, which was once a place of passing boredom, became a shelter from a home that no longer felt stable. Hard wooden seats, Billy's poking and pinching, and the worn pages of my math book reminded me that ordinary would always exist even in chaos.

Caul and I took to walking home together again. We weren't friends but we weren't enemies. Neither one of us had the energy. We walked mostly in silence except for the rattling of a rock hitting the road as Caul kicked it, and we walked slowly. We realized that we could make normal last longer if we didn't hurry home.

Sometimes we even took different roads to slow our way. Secretly, I hoped that one would lead us back to the home we used to know, but the roads in this small town always circled back to something, to nothing, to us.

Walking through our front door after school, Caul and I were surprised to hear loud voices coming from the front room. I fought my way past unmarked boxes and unfamiliar faces to find people pressed together searching through boxes and yelling out prices. Weakened, I watched as folks who didn't care enough to stand by Daddy's graveside coldly dug through his belongings.

The room began to shrink as it spun, making me feel unsteady. Stumbling, I bumped into a man with skin as thick and white as candle wax. Looking down at me, he said, "Great! You kids are finally home. We need some help with these boxes." He ran his sweaty hands over his head, which was a tangle of stringy hair combed, crisscrossed to cover the scarcity of what was left.

The taste of his sour smell in my mouth made me sick. Grunting, he slowly picked up a box and pushed it toward me. I held the box close to me, feeling the sticky remains of his handprints disappear under my own. As his fat hand came close to my cheek threatening to touch me, he said, "You sure are a pretty one, ain't ya?" Twisting my body from him, I knocked into Caul. Expecting to be pushed back I was surprised when Caul grabbed my arm and pulled me away as the man snickered.

Caul and I were caught in the middle of people bartering for Daddy's boots and boxing up his clothes. Blocked by piles heaped and stacked high, we were trapped until Denny pushed his way past and said, "You two need to load the stuff on the porch into Mr. Decker's truck." Before I could ask why, Denny disappeared into the swarm of people looking through and loading up boxes.

Turning to Caul, I asked, "Why is everyone taking Daddy's things?"

Pushing past me, Caul rolled his eyes and snarled, "Don't you get it? We don't have no money."

Watching as more boxes disappeared under the arms of neighbors and into the trunks of faceless people, I worried that with each tool and shirt packed and sold my daddy's memory would fade a bit more in my mind. Standing alone, I felt helpless as I watched my father die for a second time.

Panicked, I searched the room for something I could keep. Seeing Grandma Harlin's blue oil lamp, I cradled it in my arms as I ran to my room where I carefully wrapped it in my quilt. As I knelt down to tuck it under my bed, Mother said, "Give it to me." I held tightly to the bundle now damp with spilled oil.

Stepping closer, she snapped, "I said give it to me. Now!" Knowing I wouldn't win this battle twice, I handed it to her. Unwrapping the quilt, she held up the lamp and said, "Life is harsh. You might as well learn that now." Turning on her heel, she took the lamp and shut the door.

I lay on my floor until the drone of voices faded and our house was again quiet. Stepping out of my room, I heard the low rumble of a man's voice and my mother's, which sounded strange. I stopped short in the hallway when I saw my mother's back, stiff and straight, pushed close to the china cabinet.

The sweaty fat man who tried to touch my cheek was now trying to touch Mother's with his stubby fingers.

Mother turned her face as I had done. Moving his swollen hands past her shoulders, he slid his sweaty palm down the smooth wooden side of the cabinet and said, "You ain't goin' to get a better price than what I'm offerin'."

Walking slowly around Mother, he said, "Now ya know folks around here ain't got no need for a china cabinet, and even if they did they can't afford it." Circling around the cabinet, he added, "And the ladies who can pay ain't goin' buy it from no minin' folks." Mother's face dropped as if she'd been slapped. Putting his bloated hand on her shoulder he said, "I ain't sayin' you ain't good people. It's just how things are."

Mother shook off his hand, turned, and said, "The price I set is the price I want."

The fat man shook his head causing pieces of his stringy hair to stick to his ruddy cheeks and said, "Look, little lady, these is hard times, and folks can't be choosy in hard times." He then stepped close to Mother, forcing her back against the cabinet and said, "You is a real pretty woman."

Through clenched teeth, Mother said, "My husband just died."

He grinned and ran his finger down her cheek as he said, "That don't mean you got to be alone."

Slapping his hand away, Mother wrangled free and said, "I'm not alone, Mr. Mullens."

He nodded, then pulling a wad of cash from his pocket, he stuffed a few bills into Mother's hand and said, "I'm givin' ya your askin' price, but you should know that a few dollars for some stuff is only goin' save your boy for so long."

Stepping back, he looked at Mother as if she held no more value than the cabinet and said, "Besides, what you need is a man to take care of you, not a boy."

Mother folded her fingers over the cash in her hand and said, "Thank you." Slipping the money into her dress pocket, she added, "But, Mr. Mullens, this is all I'll be needing." Mother turned and stepped into the hallway.

Seeing me, her eyes fixed on mine, and for a moment I felt as though I was holding her up with only the power of my stare. The space between us held weakness, and misery, and maybe a little understanding. A tear ran down Mother's cheek, rested on her jaw for a few seconds, then softly dropped to the floor.

The only other time I'd seen Mother cry was when she found out Daddy was dead. I knew the china cabinet was Mother's prized possession. She loved the beautiful china cups and the promise they held of fine teas and a better life, so I said, "I'm sorry about the cabinet."

Mother waved her hand and said, "It's only a thing." Seeing Denny walk into the front room, she said, "What I'm tryin' to keep is far more precious." I knew then that Mother had cried not because of the cabinet but because she'd sold the last pieces of her husband in order to save her son.

PART II

CHAPTER
NINETEEN

It had been seven years since Daddy died, yet I don't think that a day passed that memories of him didn't seep into my mind making me feel the stab of a fresh and powerful pain. The wound hadn't healed, but I suppose it had closed best it could.

There were still times when the sweet and sharp smell of aftershave mixed with coal dust, or the cold, smooth feel of his rocker, carved a cut deeper into my heart than the one before. The hurt, like a cloak, covered my body so completely that it had become a part of me causing me to be uneasy in the few moments that I didn't feel it.

The cold lifted from my world only to be replaced by the warmth of spring and the growth of new life. Mother's daisies pressed against the house and bloomed, news of Mrs. Ingerts's ten-pound baby spread like wildfire, and I grew to be a woman of seventeen.

Over the years, Mother slowly resigned herself to being a widow, a role that seemed to suit her. Once in a while, the ladies from town would visit. I knew it was a part of their charitable work, and I despised them for their pity, but Mother had convinced herself that she was finally accepted.

Mother had regained some of her former strength, but her prettiness refused to return. Time and grief steadily wore at Mother like water over stones in a riverbed, smoothing down her character and wearing away her beauty.

Her hair was coarser and the cinnamon-colored strands were now streaked with gray. Her once bright blue eyes had dulled and wrinkles had collected at the corners matching her unpressed dresses. Mother, like a firefly's light, had faded.

Denny, who was always my constant companion and protector, now bore the unfamiliar face of a stranger. Most of the time, I felt like I didn't know him and the rest of the time I felt like I never did. He'd become taller than Daddy, with a slight build and slim shoulders that sat at the base of a long neck that never ceased to turn in every direction but straight. It was as if Denny was always looking for someone to pull him from this life into another better one.

Caul grew to be strong with a squared jaw and shoulders broader than boards, but his eyes no longer danced with devilish schemes and his lips no longer slipped into easy smiles. Strangely, I found myself missing the little boy who pinched dough and teased me.

Quitting school two years after Denny, Caul got a job working at Tommy Fulbert's Feed and Grain sweeping the storeroom and restocking supplies. Tommy and his brother, Tim, often bragged that Caul could carry several heavy feedbags at one time. The Fulberts' admiration of Caul was his greatest source of pride, especially since work was the only place where Caul could slip out from beneath Denny's shadow.

I felt as though I had changed the least. Most days, I still felt like a little girl needing my big brother to protect me and needing my Daddy to hold me, but I was no longer a little girl.

Looking down at myself, I saw the young woman I'd become and I wondered what Daddy would think of me. Peering into the kitchen, I saw Mother and Denny again sitting in silence and I wondered what Daddy would think of all of us.

As I walked into the kitchen, Mother abruptly stood. She shuffled from the table to the counter as she packed Denny's lunch, a daily routine that had worn her footprints into the floor. She'd never failed to pack his favorite sandwich and fresh fruit into Daddy's metal lunch box, or to apologize.

Today, just as all the others, Mother set the lunch box by his plate and said quietly, "I'm sorry."

Only today, Denny didn't head to the door and mumble goodbye. Instead, he turned to her and said, "For what?"

Taken aback, Mother stammered, "For...for..." With his eyes focused on her, she pointed to the lunch box and said, "For this." Putting her hand gently on his cheek, she said, "For you having to work in those mines. For not having the life you wanted." Dropping her hand, she added, "The life you deserve."

Denny grabbed his helmet, pulled on his heavy boots, and headed for the door. Before he opened it, Mother said, "Pot roast tonight?"

Denny said, "I won't be home for dinner."

Confused, Mother asked, "Why?"

Denny said, "I'm going out tonight." I knew by Mother's furrowed brows and narrowed eyes that she and Denny were going to have it out again.

"Where are you going?" she asked.

Denny sighed and said, "I'm going out with a few guys from work."

Leaning in as if someone might overhear, Mother said quietly, "They're not really the best company to keep. Miners are—"

Denny cut in and said sharply, "What? Tell me, Mother. What am I?"

Mother's shoulders slumped. Sighing, she explained, "I didn't mean you." Stepping closer, she said softly, "You're not a miner, Denny. This job is just temporary."

Denny's fingers tightened around his helmet. "Temporary?" he asked. His voice rose as his anger swelled. "Is seven years temporary?" His jaw clenched, he said through gritted teeth, "I have been in enough black tunnels for enough twelve-hour shifts to know I'm more a miner than I'm ever goin' to be anything else."

Denny put his helmet on his head and said, "I'm one of them. If you think they ain't worth much then I guess I ain't neither."

Mother shrank, stepping back and slipping into self-pity as quickly and easily as if it were a familiar cotton dress, she said, "Please, Denny, don't say that." Rubbing and pulling at her fingers, Mother said, "I didn't want this for you. It isn't my fault. I tried. Didn't I try?"

Mother stepped close to Denny and said, "Look at me, Denny. Didn't I try?"

Denny's eyes stayed fixed on the door. Mother put her hand on his shoulder and said, "I sold everything I could. I did everything I could." Dropping her arm, she cradled his face in her hands and said quietly, "I'm sorry." Barely above a whisper, Mother said again, "I'm sorry."

Denny's face softened, but he never met her eyes as he too whispered, "It's okay." As Mother reached to pull him close, Denny put his hand on her arm. Keeping her at a distance, he said, "I won't be out long." Assured she would win the war, Mother smiled and surrendered the battle.

Confident that she got her Denny back, she gently patted his hand and said, "I'll keep dinner waiting."

With a worn smile, he said, "Thanks." Turning to grab his forgotten lunch from the table, Denny's face again looked drawn and sad. Sinking back into the hallway, I slumped against the wall as my heart sank knowing that I wasn't getting *my* Denny back.

TWENTY

May made all the memories of winter melt into puddles of spring rain. The light breezes swept the smell of honeysuckle into every crack of the house, perfuming our meals with the syrupy scent. And every day was hotter than the one before, giving me the perfect excuse for my after-school escape.

I told Mother that I went swimming at the quarry with friends. Instead, I went to the cemetery alone and sat under the large tree that shaded Daddy's grave. Today, as all the days since Daddy died, I knelt at his stone and carefully brushed away the soil that settled into the crevices carved to form his name. I then removed the withered daisies from the day before replacing them with the fresh bunch I picked on the way.

Some days, the downy feel of the slender stems of grass beneath my legs and the warmth of the quiet day caused me to slip into a sleep sounder than any found in my own bed. But not today.

Today, I watched as others laid down flowers and tenderly touched the stone that marked their source of grief.

I went unseen. Sorrow seems to have a way of shaping itself around folks, making them unaware of anything but their own pain. As the sun started to sink and the air thickened with dew, I stood, stiff and reluctant, and headed home.

Standing on the porch, I'd only slipped off one of my shoes when I heard the loud clanging of dishes and silverware. I stepped into the kitchen to see Mother setting the table for five even though it would only be us, again.

Mother filled five water glasses, stubbornly refusing to see the empty seats. Scooping mashed potatoes onto her plate then mine, she sat and said, "Sit." As I pulled my chair out, she pushed a bowl of peas toward me, took a bite of potatoes, and said, "No reason for ours to go cold waiting." I spooned the peas onto my plate even though I thought it was strange that Mother fixed plates for people who weren't coming to dinner. She had so many oddities now that some were starting to seem curiously normal.

Mother looked at me, the shadow of a smile brushing her lips. She stared at me for a moment before she said, "I was running errands in town today when I bumped into Mrs. Boland." Cocking her head slightly, she asked, "Did you know that she's on the town committee for social events?" I shook my head. Mother nodded and said, "Yes, she quite involved. In fact, she had a lot to say about the dance for graduating students."

I stopped midbite. Mother said, "I, of course, told her you are going." I groaned. Mother snapped, "Don't even start, young lady. It's bad enough that I had to hear about the dance from that gossipy shrew." Pointing her spoon at me, Mother said sharply, "You're going."

Pushing mushy peas into a pile, I said, "I don't have nothing to wear."

Mother scowled and said, "Mrs. Boland had the nerve to offer her daughter's dress for you to wear." Mother huffed, "Like we need castoffs."

I sighed. The one thing poor people can't afford but seem to have plenty of is pride.

Seeing the fire in Mother's eyes, I knew this was a fight I wouldn't win so I said, "I'll wear my cream dress with the blue flowers."

Mother scoffed, "No, you will not." Thinking for a moment, she said, "I saw some fine blue silk in the window at Garber's."

Shaking my head, I said, "It's too much, Mother. We can't afford it."

Knowing this was her last chance to make a silk purse out of a sow's ear, Mother said, "I'll figure it out."

I nodded, fearing her efforts were fated to be another disappointment for us both.

Having lost my appetite, I stood and cleared my plate from the table. Putting my dishes into the sink, I headed to my room wondering why Mother wasn't able to accept cotton dresses, our life, and me.

The next day, there was only one plate and glass set on the table. It seemed Mother had lower expectations for breakfast than dinner. Only ever having tea in the morning, Mother sat blowing the steam from the cup before she took a sip and said, "I trust you will have an escort to the dance."

Pulling the crust from my toast, I said, "I'll try."

Mother stirred her tea and said, "This family doesn't try. We do."

Grabbing the remaining piece of toast, I picked up my books and headed for the door as Mother stood and headed for the sink. Over her shoulder, she called, "You'll figure it out." Stepping onto the porch, I knew what I had to do. I just didn't want to do it.

Sliding into my seat at school, I heard a childhood name that I thought would have been long buried with the pokes in the ribs and teasing. Turning around, I saw Billy Hawkins. Wearing a familiar grin, he said, "Hey, Peacock, how are ya?"

Knowing I was out of options, I smiled and said, "I'm good, Billy. How are you?"

He shrugged and said, "Okay, I guess."

I smiled again then turned back to my desk.

Furiously tapping my foot, I told myself, *It's just Billy. No big deal. You'll ask him, and…he'll laugh.* Putting my head in my hands, I thought, *Oh God, he's going to laugh*. I sat up. *No, he won't laugh, but he could say no*. Nervously, I rubbed my fingers together. *Oh God, he's going to say no*. Quickly weighing out whether it was worse to face Billy's mocking or Mother's wrath, I took a deep breath and turned back around.

"Hey, Billy, are you going to the dance?"

Billy grinned and said, "Why? You askin'?"

My cheeks flushed. "I...I just...I wanted to know..."

Billy playfully poked my shoulder and said, "Sure, I'll go with ya, Peacock."

Nodding, I smiled and said, "Okay, good." I turned around, facing front for the rest of the class.

Walking home, I was relieved that I had someone to take me to the dance, and Billy wasn't the worst choice. He'd grown up a lot over the years. His large size didn't seem so unsightly since the other boys had caught up and at certain angles he even looked somewhat attractive. His hair had turned from a dirty brown to a deep chestnut and, in the right light, his hazel eyes looked emerald. Thinking about him, I smiled as I found myself suddenly looking forward to this dance.

TWENTY-ONE

Standing on a stool in front of Mother, I felt like a Christmas tree being trimmed. "Stand still!" Mother said again.

Moving my leg, I said, "I'm trying, but you keep pricking me with the pins."

Mother huffed, "I wouldn't if you would stand still."

I started to sweat as she stuck more pins into the hem. My legs now wobbly, I asked, "How much longer?"

Mother sighed. "It takes as long as it takes." Seeing me roll my eyes, she said, "I've already sewn the buttons on to the back and straightened the collar, so I just have to sew the bottom hem."

The dress made a soft swishing sound as Mother had me turn from side to side as she studied each angle. Frowning, she said, "You're crooked."

I picked up the bottom of the dress and looked at my legs. "I'm crooked?"

Mother nodded. "Yes. It has to be you. I have checked and rechecked the hem. I know it's straight, so you have to be crooked."

Dropping the dress back down, I argued, "I am not."

Mother sighed and called for Denny.

Denny, who was home for a change of shirt, came into the room and said, "Wow, Birddog. You look great."

Mother shook her head and said, "No, she's crooked."

Denny laughed. "She's what?"

Mother said, "Crooked. Misshaped. Why else is this dress falling at uneven angles?" Exchanging knowing looks, Denny and I smiled and shook our heads.

Out of pins, Mother said, "Go take it off. I will quickly sew up this one edge, and we'll call it good enough."

As Mother took the dress back to her sewing machine, I sat on the couch next to Denny. We sat quietly for a bit before Denny said, "So, who's the lucky boy?" he asked.

Reluctant to tell him, I said, "I don't think you know him."

Denny smiled and said, "It's a small town, Birddog."

I sighed. "It's Billy Hawkins."

Denny laughed. "The boy you punched in the fourth grade?"

I nodded. Before I could explain, Mother dropped the dress into my lap.

With the finished dress on, I walked back into the room to hear Denny say, "Birddog told me Billy Hawkins is taking her to the dance." Now it was Mother and me who exchanged knowing looks. Probably the only thing we agreed on was our uncertainty about my date, but seeing the stunning success of her silk masterpiece, she said, "He's respectable." Under her breath, she added, "Enough."

Mother pulled a pair of shoes from a box and handed them to me. "These should do," she said as she helped me to slip on the white leather pumps.

Admiring them, I said, "Thank you. Where did you get them?"

With a small smile, she said, "They were in the back of my closet with a few dresses and some other things now useless in this life." As I watched Mother tenderly dust the sides of the shoes with her sleeve, it was clear to me that this night meant more to her than to me.

I carefully stood. Unused to walking in heels, I tottered to the nearest table. Denny stepped close and took my arm. "Maybe we should take a few practice turns," he teased. I laughed and nodded. Waltzing me to the center of the room, he turned me twice before we stumbled, falling onto the couch.

Mother scolded over our laughter, "Settle down, you two." Pulling me up, she said, "You're going to wrinkle it."

Looking at the dress, Denny said, "It's not wrinkled, but something *is* missing."

Suddenly anxious, Mother closely inspected me from top to bottom. Going through her checklist, she said, "I sewed the hem. I put on the buttons. I fixed the collar."

Denny nodded. "That's it. It's the collar. There's something missing from the collar."

Mother argued, "There isn't anything missing."

Denny pulled from his pocket the brooch he'd found after Christmas—the one Daddy had wanted to give to me.

I'd kept it in my dresser drawer since that day fearing that Mother's memory of her momentary surrender would one day cause her to wage war. "I think this would look really pretty with your dress," Denny said as he pinned it to my collar. "It looks nice, doesn't it, Mother?"

Ignoring him, she looked away. Mother could easily dismiss the existence of anything she wished to make disappear. I know.

CHAPTER
TWENTY-TWO

Colorful paper streamers strung from one end of the room to the other tangled with the strings of balloons as they bobbed against the ceiling. As the band played the Blue Kentucky Waltz, Billy offered his arm to me. Awkwardly, I took it as I allowed him to guide me through the crowd of couples dancing.

Stopping in the middle of the floor, he turned to me and said, "Should we?"

Looking around nervously, I said, "Maybe some punch first."

Billy laughed and walked with me to the refreshment table at the back of the room.

We stepped up to the small round table covered in crepe paper. A spread of sandwiches cut in neat squares surrounded a large plastic punch bowl with a little ladle that dipped down and popped back up in a pool of sweet red liquid. Billy poured a little bit into a small paper cup and handed it to me. "Thanks," I said before taking a sip.

Without a word to each other, Billy and I watched as everyone danced. As the waltz slowly faded into the sound of clapping hands, the band picked up the tempo with a faster song. Out of the corner of my eye, I saw Billy's foot tapping.

Nudging him, I said, "What's that?"

He smiled. "It's catchy."

I laughed and said, "Okay, let's dance."

Billy's face lit up. "Really?"

I nodded and said, "Yes, but let's go now before I change my mind."

Billy pulled me gently onto the floor. "Now I get my chance to see how good a peacock can dance." Before I could say a word, he laughed and spun me around. Turning me quickly, he grabbed my hand and spun me again before pulling me back to him. Dizzy, I stumbled and fell into his chest. "Whoa. Too many spins or spiked punch?" Billy joked.

"I think I just need some air," I said as Billy put out his arm to steady me.

The night air felt cool against my skin. Wrapping my arms around myself, I took in a breath far deeper than I could manage in the thick and stifling dance hall. I exhaled slowly as my head still buzzed with the sound of strumming banjos. As I ran my hands over my arms, I could still feel Billy's fingers pressed into them as he spun and turned me as we danced.

"I like your dress. Blue looks really pretty on you."

Blushing, I said, "Thank you. My mother chose the color."

Billy winked and said, "I'm guessin' there ain't a color that don't look good on you, Peacock."

Bumping his arm with my shoulder, I asked, "Are you always going to call me Peacock?"

Leaning close so that his forehead nearly touched mine, Billy said, "Let's dance." Grabbing my hand, Billy led me back into the dance hall. Walking inside with my hand in his, I felt my face flush with another kind of heat.

Standing in the middle of the dance floor, Billy tightly grasped my hands, then he gently pushed me out before spinning me back in toward him. As I circled round, my feet moved faster causing me to float about like a feather on a light breeze. By the third turn, I felt as though I'd been dancing longer than I'd ever been walking. As each melody melted into another, I twirled, twisted, swayed, and circled round the room realizing there was more than one way to breathe.

Walking home with Billy made the mile to my house feel shorter than all the times I'd walked it alone. By the time we turned onto Byler Road, I felt like I knew almost everything about Billy, from his favorite food to why he hated fishing.

Billy stopped short and asked, "What about you?"

I shrugged. "What about me?"

Billy said, "I've told you nearly everything about me, but you've not even told me what you're doing once school is over." Saying nothing, I kept walking. Billy ran a few steps to catch up and said, "Come on, Peacock. Tell me."

I wanted to sketch a life filled with distant places and fascinating people, but the only map I'd made for myself was of this town and brief escapes from Mother.

I said, "I dunno."

Billy shrugged. "That's okay. You don't need to have it all worked out now." Kicking a stone down the road, he said, "I'm staying to help on the farm because my dad hurt his back this past winter. It'll be good, though, 'cause I've got lots of ideas for making the farm run better."

Looking up at the trees, I said, "Do you ever wonder what these trees know?"

Billy laughed. "Did you just say *trees*?" I nodded. Billy shook his head and said, "First of all, I'm pretty sure trees can't think so they can't know nothing. Second of all, what do trees have to do with what we're planning for after graduation?"

With my arms out, I spun around once as I said, "Everything! These trees have been standing here forever just watching people come and go. Watching them make good choices and bad ones." Stopping, I stared up a large oak that loomed over us and whispered, "They have to know more than us."

Billy laughed and said, "Yep. Spiked punch."

I laughed. "Maybe," I said.

By the time we'd reached my front yard, Billy and I had settled into a comfortable silence. Close to the porch, we stopped. "I had a real good time with you, Peacock."

I smiled and said, "Me too."

Billy winked and said, "I'd a never thought that the girl who had a great right hook could also dance."

Blushing, I said, "I guess there's a lot about me you don't know."

Billy said, "I wouldn't mind taking the time to find out." Then leaning in, his lips nearly brushed mine when the sound of raspy coughing startled us both.

We looked up onto the dark porch to see Denny slowly rocking back and forth on the porch swing as he drank from a dark bottle. Billy stammered, "Hi…hi, Denny."

Denny lifted his chin in a half nod then said to me, "It's late, Birddog."

I stepped back from Billy and said, "I'll see you at school."

He smiled and said, "Sure."

I'd reached the top of the steps before I called out, "Thanks."

He waved as he headed down the road, disappearing into the darkness.

I put my hand on the doorknob to go in when Denny asked, "Did you have an okay time?"

Without turning, I said quietly, "Mmm-hmm." As I closed the door and stood in the empty kitchen, I realized that for the first time in a long time things were okay. I was okay.

TWENTY-THREE

I stood in the farthest corner of the kitchen as I tried to avoid being run over by Mother, who thundered through like a storm. "Why are you just standing there?" she demanded as she slammed a pan against the stove before scooping up five teacups, which clinked and rattled as she zigzagged her way to the table.

"I'm trying to not get run over," I said as I backed closer to the wall.

Mother snorted. "If you moved faster then you wouldn't get run over. Now hurry up, and get the silverware."

Catching sight of herself in the mirror, Mother stopped midstep and adjusted her hairpins. Fussing with loose hairs, she moaned, "This heat is absolutely going to melt me." Turning to me, she added, "At least you have a hat to cover your..." Trying to be nice on my graduation day, she paused and said, "Unruly hair."

Without thinking, I smoothed the frizzy strands with my fingers before setting the table. Putting the water glasses next to each plate, I asked, "Is a big breakfast really necessary?" Mother's hard stare answered my question.

Needing to escape the heat of the kitchen, I slipped onto the porch where the even hotter temperatures of early morning made it feel more like the end of August than the beginning of June. I wiped my neck with the back of my hand. Pulling the sticking strands of hair from my damp cheeks, I looked up to see Denny sitting on the porch swing holding the familiar dark bottle in his hand.

I sat down next to him. Watching him take another swig from the bottle, I nudged his leg and said, "It's kind of early, isn't it?"

He looked at the bottle as though considering it then said, "Not on miner's time." I nodded, knowing it was best not to argue. "Shouldn't you be getting ready?" Denny asked.

Rolling my eyes, I said, "And risk having Mother try to stick a broom up my butt to get the house cleaned too before we go?" Denny laughed until he sputtered and choked into a coughing fit. Between long, slow sips from his bottle, he said, "Miner's time brings miner's lungs." I nodded. Maybe Denny drank to clear his cough or to clear his head, but either way he never let go of his grip on the only thing that seemed to be able to hold him still.

With his breathing settled, Denny said, "I can't believe you're graduating today." Slinging his arm across my shoulders, he added, "I'm real proud of you, Birddog."

I smiled and said, "You're the only one."

Denny shook his head. "No, that's not true." Lightly squeezing my shoulders, he said, "You're the only one in this family who's going to be someone."

Turning to face him, I said, "You're someone."

Denny shook his head again and took another swig from his bottle.

I faced forward again and said, "I hate to agree with Mother, but she's right, Denny. You don't always have to work in the mines."

Denny, who like our mother could ignore whatever he didn't want to see or hear, said, "You need to get out of this town."

Setting down his empty bottle, he picked up another one and said, "There ain't nothing here but mines, poor folks, and pain." Taking a sip from the full bottle, he added, "There's got to be a heap more out there than there is here."

I shook my head. "I couldn't leave you."

Looking at me, he said, "The only one worth saving is yourself." Turning my chin to face him, he said sternly, "I mean it, Birddog. You save you." Without a word, I put my foot on the porch and pushed the swing back until it almost hit the side of the house. Lifting my feet, I straightened my legs and began to swing back and forth, letting my head roll back. We swung in silence until Mother stomped onto the porch.

"What are you doing now?" Mother shrieked.

Without lifting my head, I said, "Swinging."

Stamping her foot, Mother snapped, "Stand up." Slowly I stood. "Look! Your dress is wrinkled." I looked down at the few creases across the bottom. "Get inside and take it off so I can press it." Mother opened the door and called over her shoulder, "Hurry up, young lady. You have to leave soon."

As the door slammed shut, Denny said, "See. Mother cares. She wouldn't press your dress if she didn't care."

Rolling my eyes, I snapped, "She doesn't care about me. She cares what other people think."

Emptying the bottle, Denny said quietly, "If that were true she wouldn't claim me."

I put my hand on his shoulder. "Denny."

Shaking off my hand, he gave a weak smile and said, "Just kidding."

CHAPTER
TWENTY-FOUR

Standing in my classroom, which now seemed smaller, I watched my classmates put on worn caps and gowns as they laughed and talked. I wondered about their plans and their dreams. I realized that I didn't really know them, and they didn't know me. It never seemed to matter until today.

My thoughts scattered at sound of my name shouted from across the room. I looked up to see Billy making his way toward me. Reaching me, he said, "Hey." I smiled. Billy said, "I feel like we ain't talked since the dance."

I raised my eyebrows and said, "That's 'cause we haven't." Not wanting to show I cared, I added, "It's okay. I guess you've been busy."

Rubbing his sweaty hands on his pants—a childhood habit he couldn't break—he said, "I have been busy. My dad's back got real bad again and I had to..." The rest of Billy's words drifted into the noise of the room. "Are you listening?"

Lying, I said, "Sure."

Billy seemed to guess the truth, but before he could say anything we were called to line up.

There weren't many of us but the clamor of families waiting in folding metal chairs in front of us was the proof that our graduation mattered, especially in this town. Taking my seat in the first row of only two, I quickly looked from face to face as I searched for my family. Not seeing them, I focused my attention on our principal, Mr. Gaits.

Tall with bony limbs and long fingers, Mr. Gaits shuffled and arranged our diplomas into a neat pile. I took a deep breath. One of those papers was mine. My teachers told me my whole life that a diploma meant freedom from the limits of the school walls and a future free from the limits of this town. I knew I couldn't be free, though, when what tethered me to this town was much stronger than a piece of paper.

Denny's words came back to me. Still unable to find my family's faces in the crowd, I wondered if I would be able to save myself. I wondered whether I was even worth saving.

Hearing my name, I stood and walked toward Mr. Gaits, who placed the piece of paper, tightly rolled and tied with a ribbon, into my outstretched hand. I wished desperately that Daddy could hear Harlin said with dignity.

With no one to see me receive my diploma, it seemed worthless as it rested loosely in my fingertips. Making my way back to my seat, I searched the crowd once more to see Denny standing in the back. I smiled. He was here. As always, Denny was here.

Families circled the graduates swarming into masses that I was forced to push through as I tried to find Denny.

Shoving past a large man, I felt a hard tug on my arm. Before I could completely turn around, Denny had me in his arms. Hugging me tightly, he said, "Congratulations, Birddog." Putting his mouth close to my ear as he tried to talk over the crowd he said, "I have to tell you something."

Before Denny could explain, Billy caught Denny's right hand in a firm grip. "It's good to see you, Denny."

Shaking his hand, Denny said, "Congratulations, Billy."

Billy then looked at me. Uneasy, I looked away.

Turning again to Denny, he said, "So, where's the rest of the family?"

Also wanting to know, I looked at Denny, who grimaced and said, "That's what I was goin' tell you, Birddog. Caul's gone."

I shook my head. "What do you mean?"

Denny said, "Mother thought it was strange when he didn't show for breakfast, so after you left she searched his room. The closet and all the drawers were empty." Rubbing his forehead, Denny said, "We've been lookin' for him. Mother's in town right now askin' around."

Seeming uncomfortable, Billy said, "I'll let you get a start on findin' him. If you need anything…" The rest of his words fell flat as Denny grabbed my elbow. Making our way through the crowd, I looked back to see Billy standing with his cap in his hand. But before he lifted his arm to wave, I turned and quickened my pace as I tried to keep up with Denny.

TWENTY-FIVE

We were in town before Denny slowed his steps. Leaning over with his hands on his knees, he breathed hard as his lungs labored under the heavy load of coal dust. Wheezing and coughing for a few minutes more, he finally caught his breath. Looking up at me, he said, "I would've been there on time if Caul hadn't gone missing."

I smiled. "I know."

Slowly standing, he added, "And Mother would have been there."

I nodded. "Okay."

Denny gently grabbed my arm and said, "Come on, let's go."

We made it to Fulbert's Feed and Grain in time to see Mother through the glass window, her arms wildly flapping as she stood in front of Tommy Fulbert. "That doesn't look good," Denny said as he ran to the door.

Once inside, we saw Tommy backed against the counter as he said, "I understand that you're upset, Mrs. Harlin, but I really don't know where Caul is."

Mother shook her head. "You mean to tell me that in all the years that Caul has worked here that he never once said he was planning on leaving?"

Tommy stepped aside and said calmly, "Caul was a good kid, Mrs. Harlin. He was a good worker but—"

Cutting him off, Mother shook her finger in Tommy's face and said, "I don't need you telling me who he is. I need you to tell me where he is!"

Denny swiftly stepped over to Mother. Gently lowering her hand, he said softly, "Calm down, Mother. We'll find him." Turning to Tommy, Denny asked, "Did he ever mention any place he wanted to go?"

Tommy shook his head. His brother, Tim, spoke up. "He told me about two months ago that he was thinking about going up north, but he didn't say where."

Wheeling around to face Tim, Mother snapped, "You never *asked* him?"

Tim shook his head. "No, ma'am."

Tommy went behind the counter. Opening the register he said, "He didn't even pick up his last check."

Handing the check to Mother, he said, "We're sure goin' miss him. He was a great worker, and we—" Tommy stopped when he saw Mother's face and realized that she'd lost far more.

Denny wrapped his arm around Mother as he steered her toward the door. Calling over his shoulder, he said, "Let us know if you hear anything." Mother and Denny walked out of the store as I followed close behind.

The smell of hot cement and sweat filled my nose as we stood on the sidewalk. Mother looked up and down the street in every direction, twice, as if she expected Caul to just appear from some alley or store. But I knew when Caul finally decided to run that he'd find a way where none of us could follow.

Mother turned sharply and started walking with determined steps. Hurrying to catch up, we'd only gone four blocks when she stopped short.

"What's wrong, Mother?" Denny asked as he stepped beside her.

Gritting her teeth, Mother said, "Mrs. Boland. She just came out of Rayanne's Beauty Shop."

Cradling her head in her hands, Mother moaned, "I cannot face that gossipy shrew today. Not today."

Pulling Mother's hands from her face, Denny said, "*She's* who we need to talk to. She might be the only one who knows where Caul went."

Agreeing, Mother called out sweetly, "Mrs. Boland."

Mrs. Boland waved. The big ball of curls on top of her head bobbed as she sauntered across the street calling back, "Hello, Mrs. Harlin."

Pulling Denny close to her as if he were armor, Mother said, "I hope you're doing well."

Mrs. Boland pushed back a loose curl, "I am, indeed." Looking from me to Mother, she said, "Congratulations." Mother smiled. "It's too bad the *whole* family couldn't have attended."

Mother nodded pleasantly but her smile tightened into a thin line as Mrs. Boland said, "I was surprised when Mrs. Tillman said she saw your Caul buying a train ticket early this mornin'. I thought he would've least stayed for the ceremony."

Mother shrugged.

Pouncing on Mother like weakened prey, Mrs. Boland said, "A one-way ticket. I guess that means your nest is about empty." Turning to me, Mrs. Boland, with a hollow laugh, said, "Well, at least you still got the girl." Mother didn't laugh. She didn't smile. Instead, she turned and started walking. We again took pace behind her, and within a few strides we knew we were headed home.

We sat at the kitchen table in the same seats and in much the same way as we had done the day that Daddy was buried. Denny placed a cup of tea in front of Mother, who sat rubbing her hands together as if she were cold. Without a sip, she stared at the tiny pink-colored cup as she laced her fingers together only to pull them apart again, over and over. Wordlessly, we watched her.

Pushing the cup to the center of the table, she never took her eyes from it as she said, "I didn't have an easy time carrying Caul when I was pregnant with him. I was always sick, and I got the strangest pains the doctor couldn't explain."

Taking her eyes from the cup, Mother rested her cheek in her hand and now seemed to look at nothing as she said, "He fought harder than both of you comin' into this world. He was just fine where he was." Lifting her head, Mother sat straight and tall. "I pushed for over two hours. I passed out twice." Sighing, she said, "I pushed as hard as I could to pull Caul into my life." Her eyes welled with tears as she said softly, "And he walks out of it like it all meant nothing."

Quiet once more, Mother turned back to the teacup. Without looking at either of us, she said, "I'm guessin' you'll be next." Thinking she meant Denny, I said nothing until she turned sharply to face me. "You. You'll leave next, right?" she said as she pointed at me with her trembling finger. I didn't answer. I didn't know how.

Suddenly angry, she shouted, "Are you next? Are *you* leaving? Tell me!"

Denny rushed to Mother's side. Leaning down in front of her, he took her hands in his, and then as he had done in another moment much like this one, he said, "It's okay, Mother. It's goin' be okay."

Crumbling into him, she allowed the tears to fall freely upon his shoulder as I quietly watched. We were now three. But seeing the sad look of longing in my brother's eyes, I knew such a number wouldn't last. We were each dividing, escaping, and fading away.

CHAPTER

TWENTY-SIX

We all loved Caul in our own way and maybe in his own way, he loved us back. But his absence was like the absence felt when a chair, which hasn't been too comfortable or too useful, has been removed. You notice it for a while then not at all.

The weeks since my graduation wore away and with them so did our search for Caul. Maybe it was because our days slipped by so quickly, or maybe it was because we knew that Caul wasn't coming home. Either way, our life continued much the same as before.

Without school, my days were spent trying to complete a never-ending list of jobs that Mother wrote out every morning. Dirt-stained and sweating, I swept the porch, baked pies, and cleaned a house that was never clean enough for Mother.

The only real difference in our lives since Caul left was that Denny was here for more dinners. I think he tried his best to fill the holes left in our family, but it was never enough for Mother, who would spend an entire dinner pleading with him to come to another.

"I just don't understand, Denny. If you're not working on Tuesday then you should be able to come over."

Shoving a spoonful of corn into his mouth, Denny groaned. "It's only Sunday."

Mother sniffed and said, "I know, but I like to plan ahead for shopping and—"

Denny cut in, "If you need to know now then count me out."

Setting down her spoon, Mother said, "No, no, it's fine. I'll just buy what is needed for three, and if you can't come on Tuesday then we'll see you on Wednesday."

Knowing he'd run out of energy before Mother ran out of days, Denny sighed and said, "Sure."

Smiling, Mother picked up her spoon and said, "Wednesday, it is."

Satisfied with the dinner she'd secured, Mother didn't push for another one.

Spending the rest of the meal in silence, I watched them both between bites of cold chicken and mushy green beans. I noticed that Denny only looked down. It was as if so many burdens had been heaped upon him that the heaviness made moving his head in any other direction difficult. Mother, on the other hand, constantly looked around as if she was searching for pieces that were missing while avoiding the broken ones that remained.

Denny, as always, stayed until every dish and cup was washed and put away before grabbing his hat and heading to the door. Mother, whose inability to see any unhappiness but her own, caused her to plead with him every evening not to leave.

"It's still early, Denny," she whined as he pulled on one of his boots.

"I got work in the morning," he said.

Sighing loudly, Mother said, "I know, darling, but couldn't you just have a cup of tea with me?"

With one boot on and the other poised close to his foot, he paused.

Hopeful, Mother said, "I'll have the water boiling in less than five minutes."

Shaking his head, Denny pulled the second boot over his foot and said, "I really can't." Noticeably disappointed, Mother nodded. Opening the door, Denny said, "Thanks for dinner, Mother. Night, Birddog," before letting it quietly shut behind him.

Mother spent most of Wednesday making Denny's favorite meal and pressing his clothes while I spent most of the day trying to avoid Mother. With dinner only an hour away, Mother ordered me to set the table as she swept the kitchen, twice. She then darted from the counter to the table carefully arranging the bowls and spoons in a way that I'd fail to do both times.

With the kitchen cleaned and Denny's pressed shirts hung neatly waiting for him, Mother again checked the clock. "He did say five, didn't he?"

I nodded and said, "It's only five fifteen."

Stirring the beef stew as it bubbled on the stove, Mother said, "But he's never late."

Trying to make myself feel better, I said, "It could be work."

Mother slowly nodded.

By seven o'clock, Mother and I sat silently in front of bowls filled with cold stew. No longer hungry, I slowly stirred around the clumps of beef as I looked over at Denny's empty seat. It seemed that even Mother's pleading couldn't hold Denny in this place anymore. I guess whatever now pulled at him had a much stronger grasp than Mother. Looking up at her, I asked, "Should we worry?"

Mother waved her hand and said, "In this town, bad news travels much faster than good." Mother and I jumped at the loud sound of knocking.

On her feet first, Mother ran to the door and swung it open. Denny stood on the porch. "Sorry I'm late."

Any anger Mother felt seemed to recede in his smile as she said, "It's okay. I'm just happy you're here now." Mother wrapped her arm around his waist as she pulled him into the kitchen.

As Mother turned to close the door, Denny said, "Wait. I didn't come alone."

Confused, Mother stepped back as Denny beckoned someone to come in.

Standing in our kitchen was a woman who in most rooms many wouldn't notice. Her eyes darting from Mother to me were the color of cold slate and closely set, and her dishwater-colored hair hung unflatteringly around her pale face. In any room, she would be invisible. Yet somehow she'd caught my brother's eye. Seeing the way Denny looked at her, I knew that her gain was Mother's and my loss.

Nervously, Denny made the introductions much as he'd done when Posey had stood at the bottom of our porch steps all those years ago. Of course, it had been a long time since Denny had spoken about Posey. Not since the day she ignored him on the street. I guess there was a big difference between dating a miner's son and dating a miner.

"Lizabeth, is it?" Mother asked. The girl shyly nodded.

Pulling a seat out for her, Denny said, "Lizabeth Moorehart."

So slight a figure, Mother's small wooden chair seemed to swallow Lizabeth as she giggled and said, "Well, not Moorehart anymore."

Sharing a knowing glance, Denny cleared his throat and corrected himself. "That's right. Lizabeth Harlin."

Turning from Lizabeth to Denny, Mother said, "I thought you had to work today."

Unsure whether Mother was shocked or confused, Denny said warily, "Mother. Lizabeth and I got married."

Trying to force her sneer into a smile, Mother headed into the kitchen. Calling out, she asked, "Who would like tea?"

Denny looked to me for an acknowledgment of Mother's insanity, but I looked away.

Carrying a tray of clumsily filled cups, Mother made her way back to the table where the three of us sat, uneasy and waiting. Mother busily set out the spoons and cups as she asked, "How do you take your tea, Lizabeth?"

Lizabeth softly answered, "Just a little milk."

With a hollow laugh, Mother said, "Well, how you drink your tea is all I know about you."

Uncomfortable, Lizabeth smiled weakly. Denny leaned down and awkwardly put his arm around his new wife and said, "There's lots of time for everyone to get to know each other."

Slowly stirring her tea, Mother said, "Would that be more time than I had to find out about your..." Nearly choking on the word, Mother said, "Wife?"

Pulling back his arm, Denny stood. "I know this is sudden, Mother, but we love each other. We didn't see any reason to wait."

Mother scoffed. "You didn't see any reason to wait?" Pushing her tea aside, she added, "Or to tell me?"

Denny paced. "I wanted to tell you, but there's just been so much." Stammering, he added, "With...Caul and with—"

Mother cut in, "Don't bring your brother into this. Don't bring anyone into this, Denny. It was your choice not to tell me."

Dropping his head, Denny said, "I know."

Mother took her cup to the sink, and setting it into the basin with a loud clank, she said, "I've had enough bad news. It would have been nice to have some good."

Looking over at this small girl in a brown gunnysack dress, I wasn't sure this was good news. Catching me scowl at her, Mother said, "Well, young lady, congratulate your brother."

Hopeful, Denny looked at me.

Again, I looked away and mumbled, "Congratulations." Seeming satisfied in making me feel as badly as she did, Mother came back to the table.

Sitting down, Mother exhaled deeply and said, "Well, let's get to the business of knowing each other."

Twisting the thin gold band on her left finger, Lizabeth asked, "What would you like to know?"

Mother smirked. "What don't I want to know?"

Recognizing Mother's intent to battle, Denny jumped in. "Lizabeth is a really good cook." Not a great way to start. I smiled. Recognizing his mistake, Denny corrected, "She could always learn more, though. Maybe you could teach her, Mother." Now Lizabeth's thin lips curled into a frown.

Flustered, Denny turned to me, "Birddog, tell Lizabeth about your dance."

I said flatly, "It was two months ago."

Denny nodded. "I know. I know, but she likes those kinds of things. Pretty dresses and all."

Looking at Lizabeth, whose eyes lit up at the mention of a dance, I said, "It was nice."

Slumping into his chair defeated, Denny stopped trying. Seeing Mother, with her fingers steepled, smiling, I knew she enjoyed it and I hated to admit, so did I.

Taking a sip, Mother peered over the rim of her cup and asked, "What do you love most about Denny?"

Already standing on unsteady ground, Lizabeth nervously said, "Um...everything."

Mother set the cup onto the saucer and smiled. "It's not the most thoughtful answer, but I can't disagree."

Defensive of his new wife, Denny pulled Lizabeth up and said, "I think it's best we go." Making no move to stop him, Mother nodded before taking another sip of tea. Denny shook his head. Grabbing his hat, he led his new wife to the door. As Denny turned around, I again looked away knowing that holding on to him would be much harder than letting him go.

As Denny stepped onto the porch, the gold and pink hues of evening wrapped around him. As the day's light faded, I saw that the light that always encircled Denny in Mother's eyes faded with it. Denny held the screen door for just a moment before slowly letting go, allowing it to bang shut.

TWENTY-SEVEN

Since the night Denny introduced his new wife, Mother had waged a silent war that sent both sides to their own battlefield. In that time, Mother and I formed an uneasy allegiance that rested in our shared pain of Denny's betrayal. Even though several weeks had passed, I was still hurt and angry, yet I missed him. And the missing of Denny made me miss Daddy even more.

Without special dinners to prepare and visits from Denny, Mother focused all of her energy on me. The chore lists and lectures became longer as my time alone became shorter. With many days not my own, I was grateful when today Mother's attention turned for a moment, allowing me to escape.

Stepping over the newly turned soil, the heel of my shoe sunk into the soft dirt that formed the mound of a new death among old ones. I shuddered. Long stems of uncut grass snaked across my bare legs as I weaved my way between moss-covered stones. I'd only walked in four rows deep before I'd lost my bearings.

"Abrahams... Clemons..." Reading the stones like a map, I tried to figure out the right direction. Touching the tops of two more tombstones, I turned around several times, realizing I was lost. I couldn't understand how I could so quickly forget the path I'd worn to Daddy's graveside. Tired, I stopped for a moment. Inhaling the humid air perfumed with fresh flowers, I remembered that I hadn't picked any daisies. "Damn," I muttered.

I cut between the Denley family plot as I muttered again, "Damn. Damn."

Turning toward a grove of oak trees, I heard my word echoed back to me. "Damn. Damn." Looking both right and left, I saw no one. Taking another step, I heard for a second time, "Damn."

Quietly, I called, "Hello?" Nothing. Louder, I called, "Hello?" I slowly turned around.

"Hi! I's Diggs!" Startled, I screamed. A man who looked to be about Denny's age but with the curious and innocent eyes of a boy stood about two feet in front of me. "I's Diggs." He smiled. Pushing his tongue against the wide gap between his two front teeth, he smiled wider before patiently repeating, "I's Diggs."

Before I could answer, a man was at Diggs's side. Handsome and several inches taller than Diggs, he turned to him and said, "I told ya before. Ya can't be wanderin' off." Gently grabbing his arm, he pulled Diggs toward him as he turned to face me. "I'm sorry, miss, if he was botherin' ya."

I said, "He startled me a bit." Then shaking my head, I added, "But he's no bother."

Suddenly aware of myself, I tucked a piece of loose hair behind my ear before brushing my hands over the front of my dress. Awkwardly, we stood for a moment longer before the man put out his hand and said, "My name is Samuel and this here is my older brother, Jedidiah."

Smiling, I shook his hand before Diggs pushed into me causing me to stumble backward. "I's Diggs!" he shouted.

Pulling me to my feet, Samuel said, "I'm sorry." Turning to his brother, Samuel corrected, "You got to be careful."

Diggs pushed close to him and said again loudly, "I's Diggs."

Samuel sighed. "I know. I know, but that's your nickname."

Turning to Diggs, I said, "I have a nickname too. It's Birddog."

Nodding, Diggs grinned.

Samuel repeated, "Birddog?"

I laughed. "Yep. My brother started calling me Birddog when I was little, and it stuck."

Samuel smiled. "My mama told me that I couldn't say 'Jedidiah' when I was little, so I started callin' him Diggs."

Watching as Samuel lovingly rubbed the top of Diggs's head, I asked, "But why *Diggs*?"

Samuel laughed. "It's 'cause that's all he does. He loves to dig. He's dug up our whole yard more than I can count and our neighbor's yard too." Serious, he added, "That only happened once."

Listening to Samuel, Diggs tugged on his sleeve and pointed. Samuel smiled and nodded. "Sure." Diggs clapped his hands twice before heading toward a small tool shed.

Calling after him, Samuel said, "Just stay where I can see ya."

We watched as Diggs settled himself on his knees to scoop out the first handful of soft dirt. He wore a plaid shirt, untucked, with chocolate-colored baggy pants rolled high so that the cuff fell an inch above his ankle. Kneeling on the ground, his bare feet stuck out behind him showing toes that splayed in different directions, as if they were never forced to line up straight inside a shoe. Pushing back his faded black wide-brim hat, he tilted forward to scoop up another handful of dirt.

Turning to face me, Samuel said solemnly, "My mama named him Jedidiah Bartholomew after she found out that his brain was too small for his head. She figured if his name was big nobody would notice that his brain wasn't."

Samuel looked at Diggs and said, "I suppose she was evenin' out the odds, but God already done that when he made Diggs's heart bigger than most." Seeing how much Samuel loved Diggs, I figured God evened the odds when he gave Samuel to Diggs.

As Samuel watched Diggs, who quickly waved once before disappearing behind the shed, I watched Samuel. He had broad shoulders with strong arms that curved as he hooked the tips of his thumbs into his pockets. His eyes were an earthen brown with flecks of gold that flickered when he smiled, which he was quick to do and often, and his jaw was strong and tight-set, jutting forward with determination. Undeniably, Samuel was handsome, but what drew me to him was his kindness.

Feeling me stare, Samuel slowly turned, shifting his shoulders only slightly as if he'd never faced in any direction but mine. "Is something wrong?"

Blushing, I looked in Diggs's direction and said, "I was just wondering if he should be digging holes." Waving my arm in front of me, I said, "Here." I added, "It just seems the point is to keep the holes covered." Samuel chuckled.

"There ain't nothin' back there except some patchy grass and a tree that can't seem to grow taller than my shoulders." Turning, he pointed to Diggs's most recent work and said, "He don't dig much deeper than a rabbit hole." Turning back to face me again, he added, "I cover them up before we leave." Smiling, he shook his head and said, "He just digs them up again the next day."

"Do you come every day?" I asked.

Samuel nodded. "I'm the caretaker, and I bring Diggs along so our mama can get some cookin' and cleanin' done without worryin' about Diggs wanderin' off." I nodded. "It's worked out really good. I like the company and our vegetables are finally growin' now that he ain't diggin' 'em up."

I laughed then asked, "What does a cemetery caretaker do?"

Samuel cocked his head for a moment and said, "I trim the grass, cut back the weeds, fix what needs fixin'. Mostly, though, I guess I mow lawns for dead people." Shuffling his feet, Samuel asked, "What do you do here?"

Knowing the words still catch in my throat, I took a deep breath and said, "I come to visit my daddy. He died seven years ago."

A soft "oh" slipped from Samuel's lips before he said carefully, "I don't think I've seen you before."

Dropping my head, I said quietly, "It's be a while."

Samuel lowered his head and tilted his face to look in my eyes before he said, "I haven't really worked here that long."

Looking up at him, I said, "It's still been a while."

"You're here now," Samuel said.

I sighed and said, "But I forgot to bring daisies. I always lay daisies on his grave." Samuel nudged my arm with his elbow then walked over to a small hill beckoning me to follow. Reaching the top, he pointed over the side and said, "Like these?"

"Yes!" I squealed as I shimmied down the hill. I could hear Samuel's honeyed laugh as I picked a handful of daisies. I smiled realizing I'd never heard a sweeter sound, and now all I longed to do was hear it again.

Samuel reached out his hand. Taking it, he pulled me gently back up the hill.

"Wow, that is a lot of daisies," he said.

I smiled and said, "Making up for lost time, I guess."

Running at full speed, Diggs barreled toward us. Ramming into Samuel's open arms, Diggs hugged him tightly. Looking at me, he smiled and said, "Daisy Girl."

Samuel nodded. "That fits."

Confused, I asked, "What fits?"

Samuel said, "The name."

Pointing at me then the flowers, Diggs said, "Daisy Girl."

With an uneasy smile, I corrected him. "No, my name is Birddog."

Wedging his thumbs deeper into his pocket, Samuel said, "There's nothing wrong with havin' more than one nickname."

Thinking about it for a moment, I said, "A new name would be nice. I think it's just what I need."

Looking pleased, Samuel said, "Daisy Girl." He nodded. "Yep. I like it. It fits."

"Want to go. Want to go," Diggs chanted as he pulled on Samuel's arm. Shrugging, Samuel looked at me and said, "Well, I guess it's time."

Nodding, I said, "I should be going too."

Stumbling as Diggs pulled him along, Samuel called out, "Would you like us to walk you home?"

I called back, "No, thank you, I'll be all right." Waving, I headed toward the road.

I weaved my way between two large stones before turning the corner to see the long, slender limbs stretched across the grass. Bowed over and cradling the place of my greatest pain was the tree Mother had chosen to shade his grave. Looking down, I saw the small stone with the word *Harlin* carefully carved into it. Laying my daisies down, I thought maybe I really was all right.

CHAPTER
TWENTY-EIGHT

The last streaks of light from the setting sun sliced across our house as I stepped onto the porch. Before opening the door, I peered into the window to see Mother sitting at the kitchen table. "Damn," I whispered. Taking a deep breath, I went inside, closed the door, and pulled off my shoes.

The silence made me uneasy, but I said nothing.

Mother didn't do the same. "Sit," she commanded. Pulling out a chair across from her, I sat and waited. She tapped her tiny spoon against her saucer several times before she looked up and snapped, "Where have you been?"

I shrugged. "Out."

Heaving a deep sigh, she asked, "Do you really think that answer is good enough?"

I shrugged again.

Mother swiftly pushed back her chair causing it to tip onto the floor with a loud bang. Mimicking me, she shrugged her shoulders and said, "Do you really think this is an answer?"

I shook my head. "I don't know what answer you want me to give."

Stomping over to me, she leaned down and shrieked, "Really? You don't know what answer to give? How about the truth?"

Leaning back from Mother's hot breath, I said, "I went out."

Mother huffed as she paced. "Out? No, still not good enough." Turning, she shook her finger at me and said, "I want to know exactly where you went."

Tired of feeling hemmed in and hounded, I stood up and angrily shot back, "No! Why do you have to know where I am every minute of the day?"

Anger flashed in Mother's eyes, but I didn't back down. "I do everything on your list every day. I clean the house, I sweep the porch, I pick up groceries, I—"

Stopping midstride, Mother interrupted, "Where are the groceries?"

Confused, I shook my head and said, "What?"

Believing she'd gained the upper hand, Mother sneered, "That's right. You were supposed to buy a pound of potatoes, apples, and a small ham."

Sinking back into my chair, I said quietly, "I forgot."

Smirking, Mother murmured, "Mmm-hmm, mmm-hmm." Turning around to face me, she said, "That's what I thought." Pacing again, she ranted, "Your father always defended you. He called you strong-willed, spirited." Stopping short, she swung around and said, "Do you know what I call it?" Pushing her face close to mine, she spit out, "Willful, disrespectful, lazy, and…" Standing up, she looked down at me and hissed, "Useless."

My mother's greatest talent was her ability to cause pain with her words. It was also her greatest weapon, and she rarely held back when wielding it at me. Perfectly landing her attack, she stepped back to assess the damage. Uncertain that she'd leveled me, she said, "I should have stopped at two children."

Dropping my head, I angrily cursed myself for again allowing Mother to so easily turn me back into a frightened little girl. My eyes welled with tears. Not wanting Mother to see the pain she'd caused, I pressed my fingers against the lids to stop the tears from falling. Mother did see and satisfied, she said, "Things are going to change around here."

Lifting her chair back up, Mother took her seat at the table. Taking a deep breath, she said, "I've spent the time you were gone speaking with Ms. Tarmar. Turns out, she's in need of help with the sewing she takes in."

Looking up, I said, "I don't know how to sew."

Mother swiftly shook her head. "For being the only one who graduated, you don't act very smart." Mother took every opportunity to turn my success into a failure.

Taking a slow sip of tea, she said, "She'll teach you." Setting down the cup, she added, "You start work with her tomorrow morning." As I stood to leave, Mother said, "Early. You are to be there by eight." I nodded but before I headed back down the hall, Mother said, "It's time you start taking care of yourself, young lady."

Slipping into my room, I quietly closed the door. I lay on the bed staring at the ceiling. Every year that passed, it became harder to remember Daddy's voice, his laugh, and the feel of his arms around me. And no matter how I tried, I couldn't remember what it was to feel truly accepted and truly loved.

Turning onto my side, I pulled my knees tightly to my chest, comforting myself as I had done so many times before. Thinking back to my loneliness the past seven years, I realized that Mother would never understand that I'd been taking care of myself long before today.

The next morning, I lay in bed until the early morning light, gold and gentle, filled my room. Too tired to get up, I stared at the ceiling listening to the soft clicking of the big hand as it slowly moved round the clock. After three quiet clicks, I flung my right leg and then my left one over the side of the bed. Slowly pushing myself up, I walked over to my dresser.

I brushed my hair into a low ponytail before running a cool washcloth over my face and neck. Grabbing my small cloth bag, I headed to the kitchen. Not knowing what to bring for my first day of work, I dropped an apple and two slices of bread into my bag before stuffing a third piece of bread into my mouth. Setting my bag on the kitchen table, I saw Mother's note with detailed directions to Ms. Tarmar's house along with another warning not to be late. Rolling my eyes, I crammed the note into my bag.

I didn't need to look at Mother's directions since our town is so small that there isn't a house that remains hidden for long. Cutting across the cemetery, I was halfway to Ms. Tarmar's house, which was only a ten-minute walk from the south end. Coming to her narrow dirt road, pitted with potholes and overgrown with vines, I hurried my steps not to be late.

Her small yellow house was nestled in a cluster of trees with branches that bent and bowed touching the top of her roof. The yellow may have once been bright but with weather and time the paint had worn until only flakes of its former color remained.

Standing on her porch, which was only wide enough to fit one rocking chair and a fat cat who lay sunning himself on the bottom step, I peered through the screen door. I squinted as I tried to see through all the tiny holes, but I could only make out shapes and shadows. Cornbread and the stale smell of age floated through the cracks in the door along with the sound of soft humming.

I knocked on the splintered door frame, and then I stepped to the side and waited. As I stood there, I thought about how no one seemed to remember whether Ms. Tarmar was a spinster or a widow, but it was a safe guess that she didn't remember either. Ms. Tarmar was seventy-eight and anything that happened before breakfast was shuffled to the back shelves of her brain. She did, however, have the peculiar ability to recall any childhood memory like it happened only hours ago.

As I waited, the humming became louder until the door was swiftly pushed open. I peered around to see Ms. Tarmar standing in the doorway with a muffin in one hand and a needle with dangling thread in the other. "Hello there!" She sang out the words in tune with her humming. "Well, look at you. You're just a wisp of a thing, ain't ya?" Looking me over, she added, "And prettier than a butterfly in flight." It was funny to hear her call me small since she was only as tall as my shoulders and if she turned sideways, she'd been completely hidden by the porch post.

Pulling gently on my arm, she said, "Come on in, now, and we'll get started." Taking two steps, she turned back around and asked, "You're here to help me with the sewing, ain't ya?"

Smiling, I nodded. Then I said shyly, "I don't really know how to sew."

She patted my hand and said, "Oh, that's okay. Folks don't know how to do nothing until someone teaches 'em." Taking a large bite of muffin, she said, "So, let's get to teaching ya."

Wiping off the little cornbread crumbs that clung to her chin, she smiled mischievously and said, "Where are my manners?" Pushing the half-eaten muffin toward my face, she asked, "Would you like a bite?"

Hungry from my light breakfast, I was tempted but seeing her little teeth marks, I said politely, "No, thank you."

She shrugged and said, "Maybe later."

I nodded as I followed her down a long hall leading to her parlor room.

Unlike most old people, Ms. Tarmar didn't shuffle from side to side when she walked, instead she seemed to gracefully sway. I followed her slender swinging body and the sound of her slightly off-key humming, hoping that she would soon like me as much as I already liked her.

Ms. Tarmar's parlor room was where she did all the sewing, and I quickly decided from a few sweeping glances that it was also where she did most of her living. With windows on every wall, the room felt open and bright. And even though ivy had crept up the sides of the house grazing the glass as it rested against the panes, the sun still discovered small spaces to stream in light.

Feeling as though I were both inside and outside, I slowly turned around taking in the room. Every corner and empty space was filled with furniture and every piece of furniture was completely covered with collectibles. My eyes flitted from one knickknack to the next, never landing for long before another one caught my attention.

It was clear that Ms. Tarmar's world, unlike Mother's, wasn't ruled by tidiness. Instead, her world was littered with everything she loved. Standing in the middle of a room crammed with piles of fabric and bric-a-brac, I felt welcome for the simple reason that everything else seemed to be. Because Ms. Tarmar was a woman who appeared unable to part with anything that had the good fortune to enter her life, I was grateful for this job.

Pushing a portly tabby cat off a pile of pants slung across her overstuffed chair, Ms. Tarmar said, "You sit here, my little butterfly, and we'll get started with some hemmin'." I sunk into the chair as the cat slunk around my legs before curling onto my feet.

Brushing the stiff orange cat hairs from a pair of black trousers, Ms. Tarmar said, "I do believe pants are either being made longer or folks in this town are gettin' shorter." Giggling, she added, "Don't bother me either way since as long as there's hemmin' to get done, I have myself a job." Giggling again, she put her hand in front of her mouth to keep her ill-fitting dentures from falling out. Pitching a pair of pants into my lap, she said, "I've already done the pinnin' and the cuttin'. You just have to do the sewin' up."

I held the pants loosely in my hands. Thinking she must have forgotten, I said, "I don't know how to sew."

Ms. Tarmar pushed the pants more firmly into my hand and said, "Firstly, you ain't no snake tamer, so you ain't got to hold the pants like they goin' to bite ya." Turning, she said, "Secondly, you start where any seamstress starts." Picking up a needle and handing it to me, she said, "With a needle and a thread."

Threading the needle for me, she began her first lesson. "You ain't need to be worried, my little butterfly, 'cause there ain't nothin' that's been done wrong that can't be made right." Softly sliding her crooked finger down the side of my cheek, she added, "Life's about makin' mistakes and learnin' from 'em so that you don't make 'em again."

Grabbing her pincushion and a pile of torn shirts, she headed to the sofa. Gently pushing another cat out of her way, she sat down. Inching her way closer to the light, she cursed her failing eyesight as she hummed another tune. I didn't know the song, but the peacefulness of her soft singing made me feel sure enough to start my first stitch.

My eyes stung from steadily staring at the thin strands of thread being tightly pulled through endless piles of pants, and my fingers and thumb throbbed with the strain of stitching. But, after a day spent with Ms. Tarmar, my sewing was better.

Holding up the last pair of hemmed paints to the fading light filtering through the window, I smiled. Casting her eyes over my work, Ms. Tarmar said, "Those are real good, Butterfly."

Blushing, I said, "Thank you."

Coming over to get a closer look, she said, "Real good. You didn't sew the leg holes closed this time." Ms. Tarmar chuckled until her tiny body tilted causing her to sway unsteadily on one foot. Quickly jumping up and grabbing her elbow to right her, I lost my balance and stumbled until I hit the wall causing Ms. Tarmar to laugh harder. Soon we were both doubled over laughing.

When our outburst finally settled into small gulps of air and short bursts of giggles, Ms. Tarmar said, "I love a good laugh. I always say that a good laugh is to the soul what good food is to the body." Taking my arm, Ms. Tarmar led me to the door as she said, "You put in a good day. You're a hard worker and a quick learner. Most folks can only hope to be one, but you…" Tweaking my nose, she said, "are both."

"Thank you, Ms. Tarmar. I'll see you tomorrow then?" I asked. As she smiled and nodded, I stepped out of the door as a black cat slipped in without the slightest fear of Ms. Tarmar's refusal. As I hurried down the steps, I was happy to know there was place where everyone seemed to belong.

Walking past the cemetery on my way home, I felt differently than I had all the times I'd come in the past. It didn't seem to be sadness or loneliness that quickened my step or lengthened my stride, but rather something closer to excitement, and for that I also felt guilty. Turning sharply, I stepped through the open gate, but I didn't go to Daddy's gravesite. Instead, I weaved my way around unfamiliar tombstones until I was again standing near the grove of oak trees.

Looking toward the tool shed, I saw his hat dancing down his head as he bent over one of the stones. My heart raced. I ran toward him, stopping short when I saw him stand and turn toward me. With bowed shoulders and a face wizened with age, he pointed to the stone and said, "It's my wife."

I said softly, "I'm sorry." He nodded and turned back once more to tend to her grave. Disappointed, I headed down the hill.

Kneeling in front of Daddy's grave, I saw that the grass was cut, the weeds pulled, and the stone wiped clean. I looked around but seeing no one, I sat down and leaned against Daddy's tombstone. Before placing the flowers upon his grave, I carefully looked over each one. Laying them softly down, I whispered, "I'm sorry."

My toes barely touched the first step of the porch as the purple and pink hues of twilight streaked across the sky. Standing in front of the door, I could see through the window the faint glow of light from the kitchen. Stepping inside I saw that Mother had left a small lamp on. I followed the flicker of light as it cast across the hall until I stood in the darkened doorway of Denny's room.

With her back to me, Mother sat on his bed folding and refolding a few shirts. Silently, I looked around the room. His miner's hat, which always sat upon his dresser, was gone leaving only a small circle of soot, and so were his boots, which always sat slumped against the wall.

Without turning, Mother said, "He forgot these." Running her fingers gently over the soft flannel, she added, "I washed them. I figured I could bring them to him since I don't know when he'll be back here." Cradling the shirts in her lap, Mother sighed and said, "They bought a house. It's small and in need of repairs." I didn't say anything because I knew whatever I said, Mother wouldn't want to hear it.

Looking around the room, Mother said, "Seems so strange that he was just living here not that long ago and now he's married, moved, gone." Never turning to face me, Mother fell silent. I walked across the hall to my room. Leaning against my closed door, I realized Denny was right—the only one worth saving was yourself.

CHAPTER
TWENTY-NINE

July yielded to a sweltering August. Soon every blade of grass was burnt brown and the creek's warm mud oozed higher than the water, which was so shallow that stones no longer skipped across but rather smacked and stuck straight up in the thickened ripples.

The early morning drops of dew were already dried by the time I stepped outside to go to Ms. Tarmar's house. Walking across our yard, I saw shrubs shriveled and birds that appeared too weary from the warm weather to sing. As my lungs labored to take in the stifling air, I made my way with measured steps through the hot haze.

It was exactly nine o'clock when I stepped onto the porch into a cloud of sweet smells floating through the screen. Three weeks of working with Ms. Tarmar had earned me the same freedom as the cats, which was to slip inside without so much as a knock or an announcement. Stepping inside to see steam curling down the hallway, I smiled as I thought how even a heat wave couldn't stop Ms. Tarmar from baking her beloved muffins.

Taking my usual seat in the parlor, I patiently waited for Ms. Tarmar, who was often late. Since working with Ms. Tarmar, I had come to know many of her habits. She didn't go a day without baking muffins, she was always nicely dressed and she sometimes talked to her cats with the firm belief that they would answer. Initially, I believed that the weather's turn from slightly hot to unbearably blistering was responsible for some of her oddities, but I discovered that Ms. Tarmar's peculiarities were simply a part of her, making her both silly at times and wonderfully wise at others.

Without any announcement, Ms. Tarmar was standing next to me. Swaying unsteadily to one side, she put a tray of warm muffins and iced tea on the table. She never forgot that I was here every morning, however she did often forget why. Handing the largest muffin to me, she took her pile of sewing to the sofa. Before taking a bite, I said politely, "Ms. Tarmar, I'm here to help you sew."

Giggling, she said, "That answers that question," before tossing a pair of pants onto my lap.

Ms. Tarmar pushed her muffin aside as she placed her pincushion in her lap, and tiny crumbs tumbled to the floor where the cats greedily devoured them before wobbling away to nap. As we sat sewing, the room was quiet except for the sound of ice clinking against our glasses and the cats purring.

"I had me the funniest pig. That little thing followed me around like I was its mama." Ms. Tarmar giggled recalling her pet pig. Ms. Tarmar always began her stories the same way—out of nowhere and on the farm. Although her stories were simple, she had a unique way of weaving wisdom into them.

For weeks, I'd listened as she skillfully sketched her stories, creating pictures so clear that I escaped her parlor for a moment becoming her playmate of seven or a girlhood friend sharing a secret. In our time together, she fondly told me about her childhood love of spiced cookies and cloud watching and her love for dances and men with wavy hair. Even though Ms. Tarmar repeated the same stories many times, she told them so wonderfully that I always listened as if it were the first time I'd heard them.

Threading her needle, she said, "Did I tell you that I grew up on a farm?"

Hiding my smile, I said, "You may have mentioned it before."

Nodding, she made her first stitch as she said, "I was eleven years old when our biggest pig birthed her first litter. Seven piglets. I was so excited that I was out to the barn before the rooster crowed."

Pulling her thread through the material in her lap, she said, "I'd just come round the horses' stalls when I heard screamin'." Ms. Tarmar shuddered. "Sounded just like a person being murdered. Well, I ran as fast as I could to the pigs' pen." Ms. Tarmar put her hand over her mouth, swallowed hard, and said, "When I got there I saw that mama pig a'eatin' them piggies right up like they were breakfast."

Putting her needle down, Ms. Tarmar shook her head and said, "I always knew people could do terrible things to one another, but I'd always figured it was different with animals."

Covering my own mouth as I felt my muffin threatening to come back up, I asked, "What did you do?"

With her jaw set, she said, "I grabbed a garden rake and beat on that big ol' mama pig until she let go."

Hesitantly, I asked, "Were they..."

Ms. Tarmar jumped in. "Dead?" Slowly nodding, she said, "Yep. Except for one."

Setting my own sewing down, I asked, "What did you do with him?"

Ms. Tarmar smiled. "I kept him." She took a sip of tea and said, "I figured if that little fellow could make it through such a rough start in life then he deserved some help along the rest of the way."

Settling back into our seats, we took up our sewing once more. Several minutes passed quietly before Ms. Tarmar said, "Baby sure loved to be warm." Pulling out my last stitch, I waited and after another minute, she said, "I made him up a bed behind the cook stove and fed him until he fattened up." Chuckling, she said, "Daddy used to tease me that if he got any closer we'd have roasted pig for dinner." Caught up in her memory, Ms. Tarmar softly shook her head and said, "I sure did love that little pig."

Scooping up a pile of shirts, Ms. Tarmar grabbed her button box and sat back on the sofa to sew. Again, I waited for the rest of the story. I waited thirty minutes, but Ms.

Tarmar seemed to have no more to say. So I asked, "What happened to your little pig?"

Tapping her glasses, she said, "Sewing dulls the eyes, dear." Seeing my confusion, she explained, "I sold him for a pair of glasses." Wiping away a single tear from her cheek, she said, "It makes the eyes water too."

After a few more stitches, Ms. Tarmar said, "Sometimes in life you have to trade what you want for what you need." Sighing, she slipped her glasses off and laid them on the table leaving, for a moment, the sad reminder of her loss until her need made them necessary once more.

Standing, Ms. Tarmar groaned and stretched. I'd just threaded my needle to hem another pair of pants when she said, "I think that's enough for today." Seeing me look at the clock, she said, "I know it's early, but it's too hot to be workin' a full day." Taking the pants from my lap, she winked and said, "Besides, you don't want to keep that young man waitin'."

Before standing and shaking loose the stiffness, I said, "There's no young man waitin' on *me*."

Taking my hand, Ms. Tarmar pulled me to my feet and said, "Oh, Butterfly. Pretty girls like you always have a young man waitin'." Blushing, I argued but she just said, "Shush, shush," as she walked me to the door. Stepping onto the porch, the black cat scurried past and slipped beneath the rocker. Heading down Ms. Tarmar's road, I wished a young man was waiting. I wished it was Samuel.

CHAPTER
THIRTY

I was halfway to the cemetery when I saw them. With his arms flapping and his feet flying, clouds of dust puffed around Diggs's pants as he ran toward me calling out, "Daisy Girl. Daisy Girl." Sliding to a stop, he said, "I's Diggs," before flinging his arms around me in a tight hug.

Before I could say hello, Samuel was at our side gently pulling Diggs away from me. "Gentle, remember? Gentle." Diggs nodded before running to the nearest dirt pile.

Samuel watched Diggs for a moment before turning back to me. "I'm real sorry 'bout that. He just really seems to have taken to you."

I smiled. "I've taken to him too."

Sliding his foot across the dirt in front of him, Samuel asked, "What are ya doin' out here?" Starting again, he stammered, "Not...not that you can't be or that you shouldn't be."

Smiling, I said, "I'm walking home." Pointing back toward Ms. Tarmar's house, I said, "I have a job working for Ms. Tarmar."

Samuel asked, "Are you done workin' for today?"

I said, "Ms. Tarmar said it's too hot to work." Shrugging my shoulders, I added, "So I guess I am."

I asked Samuel, "Are you done working today?"

Bobbing his head, he said, "This heat's burned the grass so low ain't no need to mow it." Tilting his head toward his brother, he said, "Me and Diggs decided to take the day off to go to Calvers Creek."

Hearing Samuel, Diggs rolled over, spat dust out of his mouth and sputtered, "Creek. Creek." Then he stood unsteadily for a moment before bounding toward us chanting, "Creek."

Grabbing my hand, Diggs pulled me down the road as he sung, "Daisy Girl. Creek. Daisy Girl. Creek."

Samuel called, "Slow down, Diggs," before running a few steps to catch up. Grabbing his arm, he pulled Diggs toward him and said sharply, "You can't just pull people."

Dropping his head, Diggs said, "Go. Daisy Girl, go."

Samuel's face quickly softened into a smile. Putting his arm around his brother, he said gently, "We have to ask her, Diggs." Turning to me, Samuel asked shyly, "Would you like to...?"

Smiling, I said, "Yes!" before Samuel finished his sentence.

Comfortably quiet, the three of us walked until we reached the path to Linden Woods. Turning onto the tree-lined trail, Samuel and I kept a set pace as we listened to Diggs chatter to the birds and sing. The trail to Calvers

Creek was covered with vines and weeds so that only those who knew the way well could find it.

Walking along the path as if it was another way home, Samuel and Diggs climbed over fallen trees and weaved around plants that poked up from the underbrush. I carefully followed until we all stood surrounded by trees with trunks that seemed to reach into the sky before scattering into hundreds of crooked branches.

Samuel waved for me to catch up as I stopped to breath in the sweet scent of blackberries that lingered beneath the sharp smell of damp soil. We finally reached Calvers Creek, which was nestled deep within the woods. A canopy of weeping willow branches stretched across the gently flowing water until their delicate leaves touched the willows waiting on the other side cradling the creek in their grasp.

As Samuel carefully cleared a spot for me to sit, he apologized for not bringing a blanket. Pointing to patch of downy grass, I said, "This is perfect." Dropping my bag, I sat on the creek bank.

Dropping beside me, Samuel called to Diggs, "Don't go far." Diggs gave a quick thumbs-up before plopping down into a big mound of mud at the water's edge.

Samuel and I sat in silence. The only sound between us was the faint splash of the stones he skipped across the shallow water. I watched as each one skipped once then sunk before barely causing a ripple. As I stretched my legs in front of me, I leaned back allowing the coolness of the woods to wrap around me. "Do you know there's times when this here water rises without no rain?"

Startled, I sat up and said, "What?"

Skipping another stone, he said, "Some folks say that it rises because of the willows' tears."

Looking at Samuel, I asked, "Do you think the trees cry?"

He shrugged. "I dunno. Do you?"

Thinking about the trees that lined the road to my house, I said, "I like to think that they listen. I like to think they have secrets, you know?"

Samuel nodded as his lips slipped into a smile. "My mama says that willows weep because of all the pain in the world."

Sighing, I asked, "So they weep for us?"

Samuel said, "Maybe." He added, "Mama says everyone's got to put their grief somewhere. Maybe a tree is as good a place as any."

Pulling my legs in, I wrapped my arms around them and said, "I don't see why someone can't just do their own crying."

Thinking about it for a moment, Samuel said softly, "I think that sometimes things are so sad, everything around you feels the pain." Looking up at the willows, he said, "Maybe these trees just feel it more." Tilting my head toward the long, leaning limbs of the willows as they bent and bowed toward the bank, I wondered if they had ever wept for Daddy or Mother or Denny or Caul or me.

With his knees deep in the mud, Diggs tunneled into the side of the creek bed. Because of the slope, every scoop of mud he took out was quickly filled in with more mud as it oozed down covering the hole. Even though he waged a war he'd never win, he simply started again, patiently pushing the mud aside so that whatever was buried beneath could surface once more.

Caught up in digging, he was soon so near the creek's edge the water lightly lapped at the soles of his feet. Concerned, I asked Samuel, "Can he swim?" Samuel shook his head. "Maybe you should tell him to move back some." Never taking his eyes from Diggs, Samuel said, "He won't so much as stick his big toe in the water."

I asked, "Are you sure?"

Samuel nodded. As Samuel turned toward me, there was a shadow of sadness on his face I hadn't seen before and looking into his eyes, I saw a familiar pain.

"My daddy and Diggs loved to go fishin' together. They'd go every Saturday mornin'. I was too young to go with 'em so I always stayed home with Mama." As Samuel started his story, his voice was the only sound other than the soft sloshing of mud squishing between Diggs's fingers as they both started once more to uncover what was buried. "The last day they went fishin', Diggs was nine years old. I remember he was so excited." Samuel smiled at the memory.

"Daddy said they'd be home in time for dinner." Samuel's smile slipped as he said, "But they weren't." Staring into the woods, he said, "I can still remember the smell of pork chops sizzlin' in the fryin' pan." Turning to look at Diggs, Samuel smiled as he said, "Mama always made chops 'cause they never brought home any fish." I laughed. Glancing at me, he said, "Oh, they caught 'em, but Diggs always made Daddy let 'em go."

Rubbing his hands together like he was cold, Samuel said, "Soon those pork chops was as black as the night sky, and they still wasn't home. I knew there was trouble when Mama started pacin' the floor. It wasn't long before I was sittin' at Mrs. Rawls's kitchen table, and Mama was headin' to the creek with Mr. Rawls carryin' his shotgun." I lightly put my hand on Samuel's arm. Flinching, he pulled away. "Sorry," he mumbled.

"It's okay," I said as I urged him to go on.

Taking a deep breath, he said, "The next mornin' I overheard Mr. Rawls tell his wife when they found Diggs he was just sittin' on the creek bank covered in mud and starin'. When Mama asked him where Daddy was, Diggs told her the angels took him home. Mr. Rawls said that's when Mama took off into the creek wading through the murky water wailin' for her husband." Samuel shuddered. "They found him about half mile downstream. His foot had gotten wedged on a log."

Like with Ms. Tarmar, I waited for Samuel to finish his story, but he didn't. Instead he said, "After that Diggs stopped talkin' except for a few words here and there." Nodding toward the creek, Samuel added, "And he don't ever go too close to the water." I again tried to put my hand on

Samuel's arm only this time when I did he didn't pull away, instead he clasped my hand in his as he whispered, "Thank you." Turning to face me, he said, "I know I didn't know my Daddy as long as you knew yours but..."

I stopped him. "The missin' is just the same," I said.

He nodded. "It was real hard on Mama for a long time. Still is, I guess. After that day, I tried to make it easier for her by lookin' after Diggs." With our palms pressed tightly together, Samuel squeezed my hand and said, "Truth is Diggs makes it easier for me."

I smiled. Looking at Samuel, I finally realized why the dark shadows around his eyes were familiar. It was the same look that appeared in Denny's eyes after Daddy died—a look that came from life making him a man when he wasn't near done being a boy. Turning my eyes from his, I looked up into the willows as they swayed together and swung apart, and I thought how all the willows in the world couldn't cry enough tears for the sadness most folks feel.

The hurt in Samuel's story hung heavily over me, haunting me even as I stood alone in the dark, empty kitchen. As my eyes adjusted to the darkness, I saw the moonlight shining through the shutters. Stepping over the pale strips of light that fell across the floor, I walked into the hallway.

Once inside, I looked around and realized Denny's home felt no more comfortable than the one I left. Leading me to the kitchen, Lizabeth said, "Your mother told me that you might be stopping by for a visit, so I prepared a little extra for dinner." Gesturing toward a chair, she said, "Sit." Hurrying to the oven, she opened the door and said over her shoulder, "I hope you like fried chicken and potatoes."

Although I didn't care for fried chicken, I said politely, "Yes. It smells good."

Placing her oven mitt on the counter, Lizabeth said, "Denny and I have been hoping you'd stop by sometime, but we understand that you've been very busy working for Ms. Tarmar. Every day but Sunday, your mother says."

I nodded and said, "Mostly, I hem pants."

Lizabeth nodded and murmured, "Mmm-hmm."

I added, "Folks are getting shorter." Uncertain whether what I said was true or if it was supposed to be funny, she sort of smiled as she placed a glass pitcher of sweet tea on the table.

Pulling out the chair across from me, Lizabeth sat, then carefully looking me over for a minute, she said, "Denny will be happy to see you and surprised. Your mother only told me this mornin' that you were coming, so I wasn't able to tell him." Sighing, she said, "He leaves before the sun is up and he comes home after the sun is down." Shaking her head, she added, "I don't think he's seen the light of day in weeks."

Rattling the ice around in her glass, she glanced at the clock and said, "I did think, however, that he would be home before now."

I thought back to the times when Daddy had gone months without seeing the sun. It was just a part of being a miner, but it seemed to be a part that Lizabeth didn't know. And by the sound of the breath she forced through her clenched teeth, it was a part she didn't like.

Lizabeth sighed, quickly rattling the ice around in her glass as she glanced at the clock and said, "He said that tonight he would be home at six o'clock, so I thought we would eat dinner then." Looking at the clock again, Lizabeth impatiently waited for the second hand to sweep past five thirty. As she watched the clock, I watched her.

She seemed different. Although still the color of dirty dishwater, her hair no longer hung in loose and untidy pieces. Instead, she combed it neatly back into a small bun, which she fastened with pretty blue pins. She had also traded her drab brown dress for a bright yellow one, and even though the color didn't flatter her sallow skin, it did make it less noticeable.

I continued to study Lizabeth from top to bottom as I tried to take in all the changes that made her seem so different from when she sat at our kitchen table. Feeling me stare, she turned her gaze from the clock to me. Smiling awkwardly, I said, "I like your hair like that."

Nervously fluttering her fingers to her bun, she said, "I thought it was a style more suited to being a wife."

I shrugged and said, "Well, it suits you."

Twisting her wedding band around her finger, red from the well-practiced habit, she said, "Denny hasn't noticed."

I said, "I don't think hairstyles are something most men pay attention to."

Looking down at the table, she said quietly, "He used to."

Shifting in my chair, I said, "Well, my brother is someone who—"

Not wanting to hear an argument, especially in defense of my brother, Lizabeth stood abruptly and said, "I hope that the chicken doesn't taste tough from being in the warmer too long." Opening the oven to check, she closed the conversation.

Feeling suddenly uncomfortable, I stared at the thin cracks in my ice cubes wishing I could crawl inside. In an effort to break the awkward silence, I said, "I really appreciate the invitation to dinner." Seeing the torn wallpaper and scuffed floors, I added, "Especially since I'm sure you've been really busy with the house."

Lizabeth sighed. "It has been challenging." Quickly looking from one corner to the next, she said, "As I am sure you can see, this house needs a lot of care, and we really haven't had the time."

Wrapping her fingers tightly around the back of her chair, she said, "Well, to be more exact, *Denny* hasn't had the time." Her fingers whitened with her grip as she said through gritted teeth, "It would be a grand and glorious castle if promises could make repairs." In that moment, it became clear to me that Lizabeth, like Mother, held high and often impossible expectations. And I knew that Denny, like Daddy, would spend a lifetime trying to fulfill them.

Glaring at the clock, Lizabeth said, "I knew he wouldn't be home in time. He never is."

Trying to help, I said, "It is only a few minutes past."

Turning from the clock, Lizabeth now glared at me. "Don't you think it's important to keep your word? After all, he was the one—" Lizabeth was cut short by the screeching sound of the door as it swung open on its rusted hinges. "Finally," she muttered under her breath as she stormed out of the kitchen.

I stayed seated, listening to her stomp down the hall. I now knew how Lizabeth was different. It wasn't the hairpins or the dress. It was that she no longer seemed small. Waiting alone in the kitchen, I worried about what I would say to Denny when I saw him. After all, I had nothing to say to him the night he'd introduced his new wife.

I hadn't wanted to come today, but Mother forced me threatening that she would talk to Ms. Tarmar to demand she give me a day to visit my brother. The truth was that I spent most of my afternoons with Samuel and Diggs, but not wanting Mother to find out I promised I would visit. Willing to sacrifice almost anything to save my time with Samuel, I sat in Denny and Lizabeth's hot, cramped kitchen listening to their whispered words swell into angry tones and sharp remarks.

"I'm really sorry I'm late."

Trying to keep her voice low, Lizabeth snapped, "Well, 'sorry' isn't going to make dinner less cold and 'sorry' doesn't fix the floor or paint the walls." The pitch of her voice turned sharp as she added, "Sorry doesn't fix broken promises." I was surprised how quickly Lizabeth could turn Denny's heartfelt words into a hollow excuse, which she refused to accept.

Denny softly pleaded, "Please, Lizzy, try to understand. I'm doing the best I can."

Lizabeth said coolly, "This is your best?"

Neither said anything for a few seconds. Breaking the silence, Lizabeth exhaled sharply and said, "I'm sorry, but I'm sick of the warped floorboards and the broken sink. I'm sick of the torn wallpaper and…" More quietly, she said, "I'm sick of being here alone all the time."

Kindly, Denny said, "I know. But, Lizzy, I work so much so that I can one day buy those nice things for you that I know you want."

Lizabeth huffed, "So it's *my* fault that you're never home?"

I heard the fatigue in Denny's voice as he said, "Lizabeth, please, I need for you—"

Cutting him short, she said, "We'll discuss this later, I don't want to talk about it with your sister here."

Excitedly, Denny asked, "Birddog is here?"

Slowly I stepped into the room.

Seeing me, Denny smiled. "Hey, Birddog, I didn't know you were comin' over."

Lizabeth cut in, "I would have told you, but I didn't know either until today." I lowered my head, quietly cursing Mother as I wished to be anywhere but here.

Denny said, "That don't matter." Looking at me, he added, "You're welcome here anytime." I looked up at Denny. His eyes appeared darker and his face, older.

Denny groaned softly as he pulled his heavy, soot-covered boots from his feet before dropping them to the floor beside him.

"Really, Denny? I've asked so many times to take those filthy boots off outside."

Slowly nodding, he said, "I know. I know. I'm sorry."

As Denny opened the door to put his boots on the porch, Lizabeth twisted around to me and said, "See what I mean?" I saw far more than she knew, but I simply shrugged.

Straightening her shoulders and stiffening her back, she turned on her heel and headed swiftly to the kitchen as she called to us, "We best eat now before the entire meal is ruined."

Stepping closer to me, Denny placed his hand on my back and whispered, "It's real nice to see you again, Birddog."

I smiled. "You too," I said.

As I followed Lizabeth into the kitchen, I looked back at my brother, tired and worn, shuffling behind me. Seeing him now, I realized that Denny, like Lizabeth, had changed. But unlike her, who no longer appeared small, sadly he did.

A draft seemed to draw up around Lizabeth, filling the kitchen with a cold that could be felt as soon as Denny and I came in. The room was quiet apart from the loud sound of plates clanking against glasses as she roughly set them on the small table. Sliding out my chair, I asked, "Can I help?"

Slopping potatoes onto the plates, she said, "No, thank you." Glaring at Denny, she added, "But it was nice of *you* to ask."

Denny said nothing as he slowly pulled out his chair before slumping into it as if he hadn't sat in years. As Lizabeth fussed with the chicken and bustled back and forth from the oven to the table, I took a moment to freely look around the room as I tried to see all the places smudged and stained with my brother's failings. And although I also saw the scuffed floors and the walls in need of paint, Lizabeth was where I focused my eyes when I thought of Denny's greatest failure.

Joining us at the table, Lizabeth said, "Go ahead, eat." Denny shoved a forkful of chicken into his mouth as Lizabeth took a sip of tea. Although we'd never been a church-going family, we'd always said grace before every meal. Daddy used to say with so many folks with worse lots in life than us, it didn't take much thinking to know why we were thankful. But seeing Denny hunched over with his head down, trying to avoid Lizabeth's glare, I realized that maybe Denny couldn't think of anything to be thankful for anymore.

Sitting at the small table, the three of us passed plates of food and poured glasses of tea in silence. Denny and Lizabeth didn't ask one another about their days and unlike the dinners of our childhood, no stories were told. Two empty chairs sat in the spaces between Denny and Lizabeth. I wondered if what was missing was children.

Denny set his silverware on his empty plate then pushing back his chair from the table, he said, "Everything was delicious, Lizzy. I am sure I will be full until tomorrow afternoon."

Still sulking, she said, "It might have been good over an hour ago, but all I'm sure of now is that we'll all suffer with indigestion from the overcooked potatoes and tough chicken."

Denny shook his head but said nothing. Hearing the lack of kindness in her words and seeing the lack of understanding in his actions, I realized it wasn't children that were missing, it was love.

Leaning forward, Denny asked me, "Guess who I saw in town yesterday?"

Looking up from swirling potatoes around my plate, I shrugged.

Denny said, "I'll give you a hint. A long time ago, you gave him a fat lip and bruised cheek."

I could see the pride he felt that day surface again in his smile. I knew it was Billy Hawkins, but I liked feeling ten years old again and I liked seeing Denny happy, so I shrugged and said, "I think I need another hint."

Denny said, "Okay. He forgave the bruised cheek and took you to a dance not that long ago."

Not wanting the game to end yet, I smiled and said, "Sorry. I don't have a clue."

Denny grinned and said, "One last hint. He was—"

Lizabeth snapped, "Billy Hawkins. He saw Billy Hawkins." Denny and I both looked at her. Neither one of us was smiling. Standing, Lizabeth began clearing the table as she said, "I'm sorry, but the game was becoming tiresome."

As she took a stack of empty bowls to the sink, Denny turned back to me and said, "I was comin' out of Saul's

188

Hardware as Billy was going in." Denny shook his head. "You would've sworn we was best friends the way he stopped and shook my hand." Denny smiled again. "Of course, if I had to guess, I would say that he was way more interested in finding out how you was doin'."

Shaking my head, I said, "How is Billy doing?"

Denny said, "He seems good. He's been helpin' his daddy with the farm. He said he's made some good changes."

I smiled. "That's nice. I'm happy for him."

Stacking the silverware onto an empty plate, he said, "You should tell him. He said he'd love to stop by and see you sometime."

Heading to the sink with the plate piled high, I said, "I would, but I don't really have time for a visit."

Following behind me with the empty glasses, Denny said, "You had time to visit us." Grinning, Denny bumped my arm and said, "Besides, you don't want to spend your whole life sewing and end up an old spinster like Ms. Tarmar, do you?"

With her hands covered in suds, Lizabeth turned around and said, "Don't push her, Denny. She has lots of time to be married." Wiping off her soapy hands, she said, "Besides there are other things in life."

Denny set down the glasses and lowering his voice, he asked Lizabeth, "Other or better?" She shrugged before turning and sinking her hands back into the dishwater. I sighed. The game was ruined. Denny was sad, I was angry, and Lizabeth was finally satisfied.

Recognizing her victory, Lizabeth put the last clean bowl on the dry board and said, "I'm sorry, but I don't have any dessert to offer."

Deciding that I'd done all Mother had asked, I said, "That's okay, I need to head home anyway."

Lizabeth muttered a quick good-night as she stacked the plates back into the cupboard.

"I'll walk you to the door, Birddog." I nodded and followed Denny into the front room where we stood awkwardly together for a few minutes before he said, "It's gettin' real dark outside. Let me walk you home, Birddog."

Before I could answer, Lizabeth called his name. Instead of answering her, he said, "I think I should walk with you." Lizabeth called out again. This time every letter in his name was laced with her impatience. With furrowed brows, he said, "I could walk…"

Putting my one hand on his arm and my other one on the door handle, I said, "It's all right. I'll be all right." Hearing Lizabeth shriek his name once more, I asked, "Will you be all right?"

With a weak smile and an uncertain nod, he said, "Sure," before quietly closing the door.

Standing on the porch, I looked up again at their house. The shutters were still broken and the boards still bowed beneath my feet, but the real brokenness lay inside. I was sad that Denny sought salvation in Lizabeth Moorehart because all he found was another prison with bars far more difficult to bend and impossible to break. Stepping off the porch, I headed home worried where I would find my salvation.

CHAPTER
THIRTY-TWO

I awoke the next morning and lay in bed staring out the window at the soft haze created by last night's rain. The delicate fog blanketed everything in quiet, comforting my restless mind as it raced with thoughts of Samuel. I worried that he would be angry with me that I'd forgotten my promise to meet him last night. I worried he wouldn't want to see me today. I worried that I'd lost him.

Rocking my foot back and forth, I looked at the clock. It was early for me to be up on a Sunday morning, but knowing I had to leave before Mother was up, I slipped from bed and quickly dressed. I grabbed my shoes, which were sat by the kitchen door, and swiftly slipped outside.

My search began at Calvers Creek where I'd promised I'd meet Samuel. Twigs snapping beneath my feet and shrill birdsongs were the only sound I heard as I stepped into the tangle of weeds. Stopping to rest for a moment, I stood on the riverbank watching the water swirl over the stones smoothing the edges and softening the corners. I picked up a small pebble and tossed it into the water, breaking the still surface and sending small ripples across the stream, briefly changing the current's course.

Reaching to grab another pebble, I slipped on the muddy embankment. Grasping a branch, I steadied myself before climbing to the top of the riverbank. Sitting on the grassy hill, I stared at the spot where Diggs had tunneled. The water softly lapped at the thick mud seeping along the edge. The gently rhythmic sound of splashing eased my worry but only for a brief moment. Soon I was again thinking of Samuel and his grief, his pain.

The sun rose to its highest peak before I slowly stood. My legs, leaden from having sat for over two hours waiting, caused me to stumble a few times as I made my way to the road. Although it had been only weeks, the path was well worn with my steps.

I stood above the stone that now seemed too similar to those that lay smoothed and set in the riverbed, changing the course of the current and causing it to flow in a new and unknown direction. I slowly kneeled. Feeling a pang of guilt for the neglect, I gathered the withered daisies in my hand.

"I was goin' put some fresh ones, but I figured you'd be gettin' to it."

Hearing Samuel's voice, I dropped the flowers and stood to face him.

"I've been looking for you," Samuel said. "Mama, Diggs, and me go to church every Sunday."

I mumbled, "I'm sorry. I forgot."

Sliding his foot across the blades of grass, he kept his eyes focused on his foot as he said, "You've been forgettin' lots of things lately."

I gently pulled on Samuel's arm. As he looked at me, I said, "I'm sorry about that too." He nodded before looking away again. Standing in the awkwardness between us, I realized that Diggs wasn't with him. "Where's Diggs?" I asked.

Even though Samuel stopped sweeping his foot back and forth, he didn't look at me when he answered. "I was worried when you didn't show up yesterday, so I came lookin' for you today. I figured I could cover more ground if Diggs wasn't trailin' behind me diggin' most of it up." I laughed. "I ain't trying to be funny," Samuel said. Digging the tip of his boot deep into the dirt he looked in my eyes and said, "It hurt me when you didn't show up."

I lowered my head and whispered, "I know. I *am* sorry."

Samuel's voice softened. "I was worried 'bout you." Curling his finger beneath my chin, he lifted my head so that my eyes met his. "I was worried because I care about you, Daisy Girl."

I smiled. "I care about you too, Samuel."

Turning slightly from me, he said, "I should be goin'." My heart sank so that all I could manage was a small nod.

Shifting his feet, Samuel said, "It's just that I should be gettin' back to Diggs before he has Mama running in circles."

I smiled. "Tell Diggs I said hello."

As Samuel turned, I picked up the abandoned daisies and started down the hill. I'd only walked a few feet when I heard him shout, "You could tell him yourself." I stopped and turned to see Samuel smiling as he waved his hand for me to join him. Once I reached his side, he said, "I mean you could come with me and tell him yourself if you'd like."

I slipped my hand inside of his. "I would," I said as we started down the worn path together.

Small towns hold few secrets and even fewer surprises yet today as I held Samuel's hand, I walked down a road I never knew existed. There were no signs or posts, just an old wooden marker with the words *Crawley's Corner* scrawled across it. The crooked arrow pointed toward a place where a world, wonderfully different from my own, existed.

Walking together into Samuel's neighborhood, we were greeted by closely set houses and crisp clean white sheets hung on tightly strung lines. The bed linens, which billowed in the breeze, caught the children's laughter and sent it swirling back into the air so that no space was empty of the sweet sound. The sharp and smoky smell of lye soap and burnt wood wafted its way around every corner and over each house until finally settling deep in the dust. The houses, built with jagged and bumpy boards, sat unevenly on flat ground. Years of wind and rain rusted the nails and warped the planks so that the fronts leaned backward and the backs tipped sideways, making the crooked houses seem even closer.

Each home was a brownish charcoal spotted with ginger-colored knotholes except for Samuel's house. Pointing it out, he smiled and said, "Diggs wanted a bright color, so Mama went to Saul's Hardware and bought some real cheap paint. We spent a whole Saturday painting." Samuel laughed. "When we was finished, the neighbors told Mama she was a fool wastin' good money and good time painting her house a crazy color." Blushing with pride, he said, "She just smiled and told 'em that life always needs a little color."

"What do they think now?" I asked.

Samuel grinned. "They like the color just fine now. They say it brightens up the whole place." As we came closer the color changed, shifting from shades of light lilac to deep crimson depending on which way the brush strokes streaked the slanted sides. While I looked from Samuel's house to the others, my desire grew to meet the woman who could grow a beautiful purple iris in the middle of dull brown brush.

Samuel led me to the backyard where Diggs hung over a broken fence post petting a white speckled goat. He gently rubbed his hand across the animal's back as he whispered in its ear. Leaning closer, the goat nuzzled Diggs's ear. It was as though they shared a secret language. "What's he tellin' ya?" Samuel called out to Diggs.

"Goat. Goat," Diggs said before swinging around to face us. Seeing me, he grinned and happily called out, "Daisy Girl. Daisy Girl."

Skipping toward us, Diggs sang out, "Daisy Girl, goat. Daisy Girl, goat."

I laughed. "Hello, Diggs," I said as I wrapped my arms around him. Pulling from me, he pointed to the goat that now ambled slowly toward us. As Samuel coaxed him closer with a bit of straw and a few pieces of corn, I tenderly touched the top of his head feeling the soft fur with my fingertips. "What's his name?"

Samuel nestled his face into the goat's warm wooly neck and said, "Goat."

Turning, he pointed to a cat lying underneath the porch. "We call her Scratches."

Ducking my head under the porch for a closer look, the cat hissed and batted at me. "I see why," I said as I pulled back.

"Yeah, she's spirited. Mama named her Scratches after the cat clawed up her arm." Samuel shook his head. "I thought Mama would be mad, but she told me that cat needed her love more than her anger."

Peering over at the cat, he said, "Mama said the cat scratched out of fear, not hate. She said 'cause the cat didn't have no fur or no whiskers that she didn't have no trust." Listening to Samuel's story about his mama, I realized that I liked Mama and I hadn't even met her.

Feeling the heat of someone's stare, I slowly turned to see a young woman about my age standing in the yard next door. A small child, sucking his thumb, clung tightly to her cream-colored shirt with tattered hems. Their eyes were wide, appearing both watchful and wary. I let my eyes linger as long as she did until she grabbed the child's hand and quickly walked to the other side of the house.

As I turned back around, Samuel whispered, "Don't pay no mind. They're just nosy." I smiled and nodded. I wanted to believe it was only curiosity, but I knew it was much more. "Come on, Daisy Girl. I got some others you got to meet." Wrapping his hand around my arm, Samuel gently pulled me toward a small slanted shed.

Hearing Samuel give two short whistles, a scruffy chocolate-colored mutt followed by a large three-legged Labrador came out from behind the shed. The dogs raced to Samuel's side where they excitedly jumped and barked. Rubbing behind their ears as he playfully wrestled them, he nodded toward a small field and said, "And over there is a cow who no longer gives milk."

Petting the dogs that now pawed and nuzzled into me, I asked, "Are you starting a zoo?"

Samuel smiled. "Mama takes in every stray that strays our way."

Watching as the dogs flopped down in the nearest sun spot, Samuel said, "Mama says the only thing worse than hurtin' in this world is having no one in this here world to help that hurtin'." Thinking about how I have hurt alone for far too long, I dropped my head.

Slowing reaching over, Samuel tucked a piece of loose hair behind my ear before gently sliding his hand down my neck. Looking up, I saw an old man peering at us from the crack in his door. His eyes met mine. Shaking his head as his wrinkled lips folded into a frown, he pulled his gray head back inside before letting the door slam shut.

Quickly pulling from Samuel, I stepped back from him.

"What's wrong?" he asked.

"Nothing," I lied.

Uncertain, Samuel said slowly, "Okay." He called for Diggs then said to me, "Maybe you just need something to eat." I smiled and nodded. "Mama's cookin' can fix just about anything."

Welcomed inside by the sharp scent of freshly brewed coffee and the sweet smell of cornbread, I thought Samuel might be right. My mouth watered and my stomach growled as we made our way to the kitchen where Samuel's mother stood over a large pot, stirring and singing. Stepping close to her, Samuel hummed softly at first until he sang the last verse in a rich tenor. The perfect pitch of their voices melted into one sound, which strengthened as the tempo slowed so that the last note was sung long and loud.

Turning, she waved a thick wooden spoon in the air, which dripped beads of beef stew onto her arm. Licking the drops, she smacked her lips and hummed a satisfied "Mmm." She then set down the spoon, kissed Samuel's cheek, and whispered, "My boy's got the voice of an angel."

Samuel groaned, "Mama."

Patting her son's back, she said, "It ain't braggin' if it's true."

Giving her a light squeeze, Samuel said, "Mama, I would like you to meet—"

Samuel's mother cut in, "I don't need no introductions." She turned toward me. "He talks about ya so much, I feel as though I already know ya," she said, smiling. Her smile, warm and wide, was the same as Diggs's toothy grin and her voice as sweet. "You call me Mama, baby, everybody does."

"Okay. Nice to meet you." I hesitated a moment before adding, "Mama." I thought it would be awkward, but strangely this maternal endearment rolled off my tongue more easily with Samuel's mother than it ever did with my own.

Mama again stood over her pot of stew adding spices and stirring when Diggs came in and mumbled "hungry" a few times. She quickly pulled him to her side where he nuzzled under her thick, soft arm. Then, stirring her stew with one hand, she wrapped the other tightly around Diggs's shoulders, humming into his ear as she lightly kissed his head.

Although Mama was large, she easily fit inside the small house, moving gracefully from one cramped space to the next with little effort. Hefting the pot from the stove, Mama poured the stew into a large bowl, which she set in the center of the table. She then placed glasses and spoons around the tiny table as she sang in time with the clanking of the dishes. Pausing for a moment midverse, Mama sang out, "It's time to eat."

We sat so close, side-by-side, in Mama's cramped kitchen that our elbows edged toward each other, yet it still seemed as though many more people could easily fit. There was a moment of stillness as Mama reached her hands in both directions across the table. We each did the same until we were linked together by folded fingers entwined in clasped hands. Mama's hand, warm and strong, wrapped tightly around mine. Her calluses scraped against my own smooth skin, reminding me that she was a woman who worked hard for a living.

We bowed our heads and closed our eyes as Mama said grace. There wasn't a sound other than Mama's sweet words until she said amen then everyone's voices echoed against the clatter of plates being passed and spoons knocking against bowls until the loudness of sound was matched only by the joy. I'd always been told that church was where you found God. I didn't know much about that, but I was certain that if God was anywhere, He was in Mama's house.

Mama passed the sweet tea as she insisted that I help myself. Ladling soup into Diggs's bowl, she asked, "Did you pet Goat today, baby?" Diggs grinned and nodded. Mama buttered his bread and asked, "Did Goat eat the grass?"

Diggs shook his head. "Too much dirt. I's digs and digs. No grass."

Leaning her head against the back of her chair, Mama laughed. Her laugh was a bellow that started deep in her belly before bubbling up and bursting out of her mouth in a thick and syrupy sound that spread across us until we each were laughing without knowing why. Holding her arms over her stomach as if trying to hold in the happiness, she wheezed, "Whew! I need to catch my breath." Mama coughed between giggles before settling herself. Patting Diggs's arm, she said, "My Diggs makes me laugh like nothin' else."

Looking at Samuel, Mama said, "And my Samuel is smarter than a whip, and you heard his angel voice." Samuel started to protest, but Mama lightly pressed her fingertips to his lips and said, "Hush now. You let your mama brag on you a bit."

Teasing, Samuel asked, "Isn't it a sin to be prideful?"

Straightening her back, Mama said, "Now, it is a sin to be prideful, but I think the good Lord don't have no problem with folks being pleased with his creations." Looking from Samuel to Diggs, Mama beamed as if God himself had sat them at her table.

Dinner was over, the dishes were dirty, and we each sat quiet feeling full and satisfied. Rubbing her round belly, Mama stood and sluggishly headed to the stove where she put on water to boil as she poured soap into a large basin. Mama then put some bread into a burlap sack, which she handed to Samuel. "You and Diggs can feed this to Goat while we women do some cleaning up."

Handing me a soft dishcloth, she said, "I'll do the washin' and you do the dryin'." She winked at me and added, "We don't want those pretty hands gettin' all pruned." I shyly tucked my hands under the cloth and waited as she dumped the boiling water into the basin. Plunging her hands into the hot sudsy water, she scrubbed each plate and glass until it shone before giving it to me.

I carefully wiped every side and edge until the dish was perfectly dry. I then passed it to Mama, who now stared at me while absently washing a glass. Letting the glass slip beneath the water, she said, "I always know when someone is in pain." Tapping the top of her cheek with the back of her hand, she said, "It settles in the eyes." I lowered my own eyes as Mama took up another dish.

"I was just a little girl still livin' at home when I'd seen a terrible thing. Neighbor woman's house caught fire. Everyone tried to help including my daddy, but them flames just shot out of every window and crack swallowing up that house along with that poor woman's only baby." Mama shuddered as if trying to shake the horrible image loose from her mind then she said, "After that day, her chocolate-colored eyes was forever rimmed in red."

"Maybe her eyes were red from crying," I gently suggested.

Mama nodded. "She sure did her life's share of cryin', but it wasn't that kind of red. It was a scarlet that just lay itself down inside her eyes and refused to go." Mama let another plate slip into the soapy water before she said, "Red is the color of rage and shame. She was so angry at the world for takin' her baby, and she was shamed that she couldn't stop it." As Mama wrung out her dishrag, she said, "After that day, she didn't feel much else."

Mama opened the screen door. Pouring out the dirty dishwater, she said over her shoulder, "She was lucky, though."

Not sure I'd heard her right, I said, "Lucky?"

Mama came back in and smiled. "I don't mean 'cause she lost her baby. That's a terrible thing. Ain't no denyin' that." Stepping close to me, she said, "Red is also the color of love and passion. She was lucky 'cause a body don't know real hurt until they know real love."

Turning from me, Mama wiped soap spots from her arms before putting the dried dishes into the cupboard. I looked down at the damp dish towel hanging loosely in my hands. Shifting my hands slightly, the towel slid from my fingers. Watching as it fell to the floor, I realized that no matter how tightly we hold on, sometimes things still slip from our grasp.

Stepping into the kitchen, Samuel picked up the dish towel and handed it to me. Slowly, he looked from me to Mama, who now stared out the window as if she was waiting for someone. "How 'bout I walk you home, Daisy Girl?"

I nodded, then turning to Mama, I said, "Thank you for dinner."

Mama smiled at me before turning back to the window. We'd reached the door when Mama called out, "Samuel, I need to speak with you." Samuel gently squeezed my shoulder before heading back to the kitchen as I slipped outside.

Mama tried to keep her voice quiet, but as I sat on the porch step waiting, I regretfully heard every word. Strong and sure of herself, she warned Samuel, "I don't think she's the girl you should be bringin' home."

Challenging his mother, Samuel said, "You're the one who says it's the Lord's job to judge and our job to forgive."

I pictured Mama leaning closer, trying to keep her voice low as her anger caused it to grow louder. "I know what I said, boy, you don't need to be repeatin' my words to me. But not everyone lets the Lord do the judgin'." I leaned closer to hear as Mama lowered her voice to a near whisper and said, "There are those who do the judgin' and the punishin'."

Samuel said, "I know, Mama. I'm sorry."

Mama's voice softened as her words again became loving. "You ain't got no reason to be sorry, but you got plenty of reason to watch what you're doin'."

Pressing my ear flat to the door, I heard Samuel quietly say, "I thought you liked her."

Mama sighed and said, "I like her just fine, but we both know it ain't a matter of likin' her. It's a matter of..." Whispering the word at the same time, Mama and I said, "Belonging." At that moment, I knew that as much as I wanted to belong—I never would.

THIRTY-THREE

As fall fell forward, folding us into her October coat of brilliant colors, I watched once more with awe as the trees tinted red, orange, and gold appeared aflame against the sky's new hazy gray hue.

In the past two months as October's brisk air sharpened, cutting a fresh clean space in September's smothering heat, Samuel and I spent every stolen moment together. We went on long walks, which winded down dirt roads and around quiet corners of open fields. Sometimes we sat silent, but mostly we talked.

We talked about our lives, the way they had been and the way we hoped they would one day be. But in all those times, Mama's words were never mentioned. Instead I buried them beneath my life's other aches, along with my fear that Samuel's feelings would change because of them.

I wanted to see us as the same—we'd both lost, felt unbearable grief and survived, each in our own way, but I knew the difference couldn't be denied. After Samuel's daddy died, Mama grabbed the tattered ends and sewed them up, tightly tying each to the other until they were enclosed inside a warm and loving home. My mother allowed the frayed threads to pull loose from her grasp, unstitching us from each other until we were left splintered and broken inside a cold and quiet house.

I couldn't tell him about this family, so I told him about the one that once had been—the one that grief had stolen. It was too hard to talk of a dead father, a missing brother, and a crazy mother, no matter how hard I imagined it differently, so I mostly talked about Denny. I took pieces of memories and bits of hope and created a brother who was still my constant companion and protector—the one I remembered.

Stepping into a pile of leaves, I listened to the soft crackling sound as my shoe crunched the dried leaves into the ground before kicking my leg into the pile. The leaves soared catching on the corners of the breeze, tilting and turning before tumbling back down.

I passed a few houses still quiet in Sunday's early afternoon. Pumpkins sitting on porches were carved into gap-toothed jack-o'-lanterns and bales of hay with pieces of straw poking out of the bundles sat next to them. As the clouds thickened and hung heavy with the threat of rain, I hurried up Higgins Hill.

Passing Widow McIntyre's house, I looked up at the large porch where her rocker now sat empty. With her gray hair and wrinkled face, she now looked like the widow she'd become years ago. Elaina once told Mother that she'd married the greatest love of her life so knowing everyone else would pale she never tried to love again.

As I headed down the hill, I saw Samuel at the bottom waiting. My stomach seemed to lurch into my chest as both my heart and breath quickened. Running toward him I knew that if we each only got one great love then he was mine.

Facing the open field, Samuel stood twirling a thin piece of straw between his lips as he leaned against the fence that enclosed the place where many of my childhood hours were spent and my fondest memories made.

Stopping short of running into him, I said breathlessly, "Hi, Samuel."

Turning, he pulled the straw from his mouth and smiled. "I'm guessin' this the barn you've been talkin' about."

I nodded, coming closer until our arms touched as we bent over the fence rail looking at the place that defined a certain piece of me.

Tall trees, bent and twisted, lined both sides of Byler Road. Burnt amber and crimson leaves hung loosely from the branches soon to be covered with winter's soft blanket of snow. I glanced around even though I knew Diggs wasn't here and for the first time I didn't ask why. Instead, I slipped my arm around Samuel's waist, happy for this moment—our moment.

Standing close, we were quiet for a while before I said, "Mother forbade Denny and me to play in the barn. She said it was filthy and unsafe." It was the first time I'd talked about Mother. Oddly, as my words moved from my mouth to the empty space between us, she seemed a little less like a large force pressing down on me and a little more of a mother who didn't want her children hurt.

Samuel said, "Mama always has a say about what I should be doin'." He paused a moment before saying, "I guess it's part of their job."

Nodding, I said, "Well, my mother takes her job real serious." Samuel smiled. "No, really. She had rules for how a lady should act," I said.

"Such as?" Samuel asked.

Counting them on my fingers, I said, "Well, I am never to partake in any activity that involves bugs, dirt, or disreputable people."

Samuel grinned. "I'm guessin' you broke a few."

Laughing, I said, "I was always covered in dirt up to my knees with some kind of bug trying to crawl out of my pockets."

Pulling a leaf that caught on my dress, he said, "I guess some things don't change."

I took the leaf. Dropping it, I watched as it fluttered to the ground, happy to think that some things do stay the same.

"What about the last rule?" Samuel asked. "The disreputable people." Moving closer, he asked, "Did you break that one?" Pressing his lips close to my ear, he teasingly whispered, "Or are you breakin' that one now?"

Placing my hand against his cheek, I looked into his eyes dancing with mischief and worry and said, "My daddy always said the wrong kinds of people are the ones who aren't good and loving." Gently wrapping my hand around the back of his neck, I pulled him close to me and whispered, "You, my Samuel, are only goodness and love. Nothing less."

The air thickened around us as the clouds swelled with rain. The droplets fell slowly at first, lightly landing on the dried leaves, the fence, and us. Samuel wiped a few drops from his forehead and said, "We better get inside. With a sky that black, it's only goin' get worse before it gets better."

Grabbing my hand, Samuel led me toward the barn. We'd only taken a few steps before the rain came down harder. Caught in the downpour, we ran until we reached the barn door. With one hand, Samuel lifted the rotted board from the rusted latch. Drenched, we stepped inside. As the stale smell of manure and straw curled beneath my nose, I inhaled the familiar scent of childhood and simpler, happier days.

Samuel shut the doors tight against the cold. With only a bit of light filtering through a small yellowed window, he said, "Let's go up into the loft where it ain't so dark." Agreeing, I grabbed an old forgotten wool blanket draped over a stall and followed him as he climbed up the ladder.

The roof was low and straw was scattered over the warped boards, but it was brighter and warmer in the smaller space. Samuel spread the blanket, smoothing the edges before offering me a seat. Crouching on my knees, I ran my fingers through my hair as I tried to pull out the tangles, then I squeezed the water from the ends causing drops to trickle down my neck and back.

I was so soaked that my skin stung from the cold causing me to shiver. Samuel reached his hands toward me, sliding them slowly up my arms until they rested lightly on my shoulders before pulling me close to him. As I sat, wrapped in his arms with my cheek pressed to his, he whispered, "You still shivering?" I nodded even though I wasn't shivering; I was trembling.

Enfolded in each other's arms and pressed tightly together, we listened to the rain softly tap against the roof. Samuel's hands, which settled onto my shoulders, moved down my arms once more until his fingers folded into mine. As he gently leaned back, I looked into his eyes and saw that they were edged in a new light that I could only silently hope was love.

Smiling, Samuel tilted his head as he leaned toward me before tenderly touching his mouth to mine. His lips, soft and slightly parted, pressed hard against my own until our breath seemed to come from the same space. Unclasping his hands from mine, Samuel timidly reached toward the top of my dress. He paused for a moment, waiting. I nodded. He then slowly pushed the small pearl buttons through the tiny holes so that the wet wrinkled dress surrendered to his touch tumbling softly to the floor.

His eyes like his hands roamed over my body before he whispered, "You're beautiful." I lowered my head as my face flushed, but Samuel tucked his finger beneath my chin lifting my eyes to meet his before pulling me close. He lay back, drawing me to him so that we slowly sank to the floor together.

I clung to him as he clutched me tighter, our cool bare skin warming with each touch until I ached to know and be known. As he held me, our chests pressed together so that I could hear our hearts beat in time with each other and the falling rain, which slowly and steadily tapped against the roof.

Soon the drops, fuller and heavier, fell fast and hard again until the rain pounded down in an unbroken rhythm causing the roof to pulse with the pressure of the water, which washed the world and us in its rushing sound. Our breath quickened and then slowed in time to the tempo of the rain until we were a part of it and each other. I lay by Samuel's side, resting my head against his chest as I listened to his heart slow into a soft beating and his breathing become even and quiet.

Looking peaceful and happy, he traced his finger gently around my face before closing his eyes and murmuring, "I love you, Daisy Girl." As Samuel slept, I allowed my eyes to adjust to the faint yellow-hued light that sunk into the brown beams casting across the chestnut-colored floor until it faded into darkness.

I tightened my arms around him so that we were wrapped together with our limbs tangled and our heads close. As I closed my eyes, I thought how I'd brought him here to show him a bit of my world. But as I lay in his arms, I realized that with him no other world existed other than the one we created when we were together.

CHAPTER

THIRTY-FOUR

The days' light grew shorter as did my time with Samuel. Moments spent with him were usually too few, often stolen, but always precious. Most of my time was spent sewing for Ms. Tarmar, but there wasn't a stitch sewn or a pant leg hemmed that I didn't think of Samuel and long for the time we would be together. Sundays soon became my cherished day when I would quietly stand and patiently wait at the bottom of Higgins Hill for my Samuel, my love, my salvation.

With my hand in his, we always made our way to the barn, hurrying to the quiet cover of the loft and the warm heat of each other. During our days together, I'd noticed how the light of late November spread over the barn settling deep into the weathered beams. Wrapped in Samuel's arms, I often wondered if it was the way autumn's light faded and fell in faint slivers across the barn or whether all the colors in my world appeared a little brighter now.

It was in those days, brief in hours but full with passion, I came to discover love again, only this time it wasn't the love of a little girl with all her foolish notions, but rather the love of a woman with all her expectations.

Night still hadn't completely pulled the cover of darkness from our world as I lay in bed listening to Mother happily humming in the kitchen. Each verse was punctuated with a pan clanked against the stove, a cupboard door slammed, or my name being called. By the third time, Mother no longer hummed and I knew I couldn't hide any longer. Quickly dressing, I went into the kitchen to find Mother still wearing her house robe as she buttered the turkey.

Her hair was pulled back but some pieces having pulled free in her sleep fell about her face. Impatiently she pushed them back and tucked them behind her ear before putting the metal basting pan into the oven. Standing, she called, "Young lady!" About to call my name again, she turned, then seeing me she snapped, "Why are you just standing there? Did you hear me calling you?"

I pulled out a chair and sunk into it. Yawning, I said, "The neighbors could hear you calling me."

With her hands on her hips, she said, "Well?"

I sighed. "Well, that's why I'm out here."

Throwing her potholders onto the table, she said, "I don't like your sass." Then looking me over from head to toe, she added, "And I don't like what you're wearing."

Pointing to her house robe, I said, "I didn't think this dinner was fancy."

Putting her hands on the table, Mother leaned forward and glared at me. "What did you say?"

I smiled. "I was trying to be—"

Mother cut in, "Funny?"

Looking down at my lap, I said, "I'm sorry."

As Mother stomped to the counter, she muttered, "Useless."

Handing me a set of plates, Mother warned, "Be careful." I set each one on the table along with the silverware, counting four place settings. It was at least a week of silent warring, each side offering reasons why her house would be most suitable for Thanksgiving dinner. But in the end Mother won—she always did.

For weeks, Mother had planned and prepared a meal that proved her win rightfully earned. Because Mother had been so busy, I'd been able to slip away every Sunday unnoticed. As a child, I would've bartered with my soul for just a sliver of the light that encircled Denny in my mother's eyes, but now as a woman I was grateful to hide in the shadows. It was in this recess of light that I could remain secreted from her and her ever watchful, always judging eye.

Mother handed me a set of glasses and a candle. "Place these on the table then go change your dress." I nodded. "And, young lady..." Frowning, she paused before saying, "Try to be less..." She sighed and said, "Just try." I didn't say a word, instead I went to my room.

Closing my door, I walked to my closet. I pulled out a dark navy dress with a thin strip of lace around the collar. Slipping it over my head, I fastened the buttons then twirled in front of the mirror. Catching my reflection, I smiled thinking how Samuel would love this dress. He said that I was pretty in every color but beautiful in blue. I opened the door, thinking that perhaps I'll wear it the next time we meet.

I walked back into the kitchen to see that Mother was also dressed. Her hair, no longer loose, was pulled tightly back into a bun causing her to look more severe in the morning light. Putting the bowls onto the table, she stopped and looked at me. "It's good enough, I suppose."

I looked down at my dress, thinking how it was never good enough. Watching me, she said, "Well, there's no time to change now. They will be here any—" Mother's final words were clipped by the sound of light knocking.

Pushing past me, Mother opened the door. Smiling, she pulled Denny inside. Denny kissed Mother's cheek before stepping aside for his wife to come in. "Happy Thanksgiving," Lizabeth said.

Without a glance in her direction, Mother said, "Yes, you too, Lizabeth." Pulling out a chair, she said sweetly, "Sit, Denny. I've made all your favorites."

Lizabeth sulked in the corner until Denny, pulling out a chair, said, "Come sit, Lizzy."

Taking a seat next to Denny, Lizabeth asked Mother, "Is there anything I can do to help?"

Mother straightened her dress and said, "No. I don't need your help." Catching Denny glaring at her, Mother forced her lips into tight smile and said, "You have done more than enough by making dessert."

Lizabeth jumped up. Putting her hand over her mouth, she groaned, "The pie!"

Turning quickly to Denny, she asked, "Did you bring it?"

Standing up, Denny put his hand on Lizabeth's shoulder and said, "I'm sorry, I forgot. I'll go back and get it."

Shaking off Denny's hand, Lizabeth sank into her seat and hissed, "It's going to be cold."

Denny looked at me, which he hadn't done since he walked in the door, and said, "Come with me." Grateful to leave, I nodded. I grabbed my coat and waited on the porch while he apologized again to Lizabeth before shutting the door. Without another word to me, Denny started down the road.

With long strides, Denny walked quickly causing me to have to run at times to keep up. I tucked my face into my coat as the wind, which circled and spun around us in small currents, whipped across my cheeks. Peering over the edge of my thick wool collar, I watched Denny. With his coat hanging loosely around his shoulders, he didn't seem bothered by the cold. But the way he clenched his jaw and stiffened his back, I knew he was bothered by something.

We were on Byler Road before I realized that Denny still hadn't said a word. It wasn't until we passed Miller's barn that he snapped, "Mother is right. That barn should be torn down."

Hurt that Denny wanted to destroy a place that for me held only sweet memories, I said, "We used to play inside that barn."

Denny said, "We ain't kids no more," before quickening his pace again. I wrapped my coat tighter around me as we walked the rest of the way in silence.

Denny pushed open the door causing it to bang against the wall. I stood on the porch waiting until he whipped around and snapped, "Come on." Inside, he pulled off his coat and threw it on the sofa before moving quickly across the length of the room. I knew from the way he walked to how his eyes turned dark that we were here for more than just pie.

Pacing back and forth like a caged dog, Denny roughly twisted and turned one hand over the other. Stopping midstep, he swung around to face me. "I know," he said. Confused, I said nothing. Angry, he shouted, "Do you hear me? I said I know. I know about him." I knew he meant Samuel, and I knew my secret was no longer mine.

"How?" I asked.

Taking two short steps toward me, Denny said, "It don't matter how I know." Taking another step, he said, "What matters is you're takin' up with him." Denny shook his head. "God, Birddog, what do you think is goin' happen when folks find out?"

Now I took a step forward. Raising my chin, I looked him in the eye and said, "I don't give a damn what folks think or what they say."

Pushing his face close to mine, he said, "Well, you better give a good goddamn about what they're goin' *do* when they find out you're running with a nigger."

217

I stumbled back against the wall as though physically struck. Sliding to the floor, I put my head in my hands and whispered, "I love him."

Standing over me, Denny looked down and asked, "What do you know about love?"

I looked up at him and said, "What do *you* know about love?"

The anger drained from his face. The lines around his eyes and mouth smoothed, softening his face back into the boy I remembered. "You're so young, Birddog. There are so many men who would love to love you." With a half-hearted smile, he said, "There ain't a time that I've run into Billy Hawkins that he ain't asked about you."

Trying to hide the tears that streamed down my face, I sniffed and said, "I don't want Billy. I want Samuel."

Denny crouched down in front of me. Leaning close, he said, "Sometimes it ain't about what you want. It's about what you need. And you need a man who ain't going bring hate down on you."

"Why can't you choose to see my love for Samuel instead of everyone's hatred?"

Denny slowly stood and said, "Your love ain't what everyone is goin' see." Denny sighed. "All they're goin' see is a black boy with a white girl."

I quickly stood and said, "It's just a color, Denny."

Denny said, "It's the wrong one."

Angry, I snapped, "Who says? You?"

Denny shook his head. "It ain't about me, Birddog."

Pointing a trembling finger at him, I shouted, "It is about you, Denny, because it's what you think that matters to me." Lowering my voice, I said, "How can you find Samuel's color—the same color as Daddy's rocker and the tree trunks we climbed—wrong?"

Denny dropped his head and said softly, "I won't tell Mother, but you have to stop seeing him. Do you understand?"

I didn't understand, not at all, but to save my Samuel I whispered, "Yes." Standing alone in the quiet of Denny's house, we locked eyes for a moment as we shared a silent understanding. His was that I would never see Samuel again and mine was to find another way.

THIRTY-FIVE

I stood for a moment on the road leading from Ms. Tarmar's house to my own. Looking around, I noticed that in some secret and unseen moment, the season had completely slipped off November's gown of beautiful colors and quietly changed into the plain and bleak dress of December.

Tilting my head back and closing my eyes, I enjoyed the warmth of the sun on my cheeks as I inhaled the crisp winter air. I slowly opened my eyes to see a hazy sky full of thick low-hanging clouds, heavy and bulging with snow, rolling and rushing past.

The wind, blowing harder and stronger, lashed sharply across my cheeks, forcing me to tuck my face into my coat so that I could only see a few feet of the ground in front of me. I walked quickly trying to warm my toes, which tingled inside my worn shoes, as I pushed my stinging fingers deeper into my pockets.

Hearing their voices echo against the stillness, I lifted my head from my coat.

Folding down my stiff collar, I saw Samuel and Diggs walking so close they could have been the other's shadow.

As always, Diggs reached me first. Grinning, he said, "Cold. Diggs cold."

I nodded before I wrapped my arms around him and said, "I missed you."

Diggs hugged me a bit tighter before pulling away to call after Samuel.

I felt Samuel at my side even before I saw him. Leaning in, he said quietly, "Hello, Daisy Girl."

I smiled. "Hello, Samuel." It had been two weeks since I'd seen him, yet as I stood close to him it was as though no time had passed.

Seeing a small rabbit bound toward the woods, Diggs giggled before giving chase. Samuel and I watched, laughing, as Diggs chased the small rabbit down the road. As Diggs settled himself on a nearby rock, Samuel faced me. Suddenly serious, he said, "It's been a long time since I've seen you."

Turning slightly from Samuel, I said, "I've been busy," before stammering out an excuse. "It's just with…with Thanksgiving."

Samuel said, "I understand. We was busy too. Mama got a big ol' turkey and Diggs was—"

Cutting Samuel short, I said, "It wasn't just Thanksgiving. I was also busy working for Ms. Tarmar."

Sliding his arm around my waist, he said, "It's okay. We got time now."

Pulling from him, I said, "I have to be home soon. With Christmas coming soon, Mother is expecting my help and—"

Before I could finish, Samuel said, "It's okay." He took my hands and pulled me close to him. "How about tomorrow?"

I sighed. "Samuel, I can't. I have to work."

Samuel persisted, "After work?"

Frustrated, I snapped, "I can't." Samuel dropped his head. Guilty, I said softly, "I promise we'll see each other after Christmas."

Snapping his head up, Samuel said, "That's a long time."

"I know," I said. More hopefully, I added, "It will go by quickly."

Samuel said bitterly, "Maybe for you." Seeing how his words hurt me, he quickly pulled me to him and whispered, "I'm sorry."

Choking back my tears, I said, "No, Samuel. I'm sorry."

Lifting my face to his, he said, "You ain't got no reason to be sorry." Tenderly kissing my cheek, he said, "I just miss you so much."

Pulling back from him, I said, "I promise that I'll try to find a way to see you sooner."

Seeing me shivering, he said, "You head on home." I nodded. I'd only taken a few steps when he called out, "We'll find a way." I smiled. Turning, I thought how the way was much harder than he knew.

I awoke early. Lying in bed, I pulled at my damp nightgown, which twisted and folded tightly around my waist. Pulling it back down, I felt my skin slick with sweat. Reaching my fingertips to my temple, I wiped away the sweat that beaded on my forehead trickling onto my cheek.

Turning over in bed, my stomach rolled and flipped causing a sick feeling to rise into my tightened throat, making my mouth water and my eyes tear. Flinging back the blankets, I quickly put my hand over my mouth as I ran to the bathroom. Slamming the door shut, I fell to my knees and grasped the toilet bowl with my hands.

My stomach muscles clenched and twitched until my body took over, forcing me violently forward as I heaved until my throat burned and tears streamed down my face. Leaning back, I waited until my stomach again seized. After four times, I slowly and unsteadily stood. I rinsed my mouth and splashed cold water on my face before staggering back to my room.

Carefully crawling back into bed, I lay still trying to settle my stomach. I tried to shift to my side but even the slightest movement took too much energy. Wrapping my quilt around me, I cursed all those long walks home in the cold and rain. Trying to stop my head from spinning, I focused on a small watermark on my wall. Tracing the dark outer edges that curved and faded, I thought about Samuel.

It had been weeks since I'd seen him. I closed my eyes trying to remember his scent, the cut of his jaw, the curve of his back. It seemed to get harder every day to picture him. As

I tucked my legs tightly to my chest and put my hand gently on my stomach, I realized what was wrong. I was heartsick. It was then that I knew I had to find a way to see Samuel—soon.

Mother pounded on the door. "You're going to be late!" After a few seconds, she shouted, "Do you hear me?"

I groaned. "Yes."

Opening the door, she peered in. "What's wrong?"

Rolling over, I mumbled, "Nothing."

Coming closer to my bed, she asked, "Then why are you still in bed?"

Pulling back my quilt, she said, "You don't look very good."

I sighed and said, "I know. You've told me."

Mother huffed, "Not in general. Now. You don't look good now." She put her hand on my forehead for a few seconds. "You're not feverish."

Swinging my legs over the side of the bed, I said, "I'm fine." Mother watched me as I walked unsteadily to my dresser. Making it across the room without stumbling, I said, "I'm just tired."

Unsure but unwilling to argue against a day's wages, Mother said, "Well, fine. I'll put some bread and fruit in a bag. You can eat on the way." Before shutting the door, she added, "Wash your face."

Mother was staring out the window when I came into the kitchen. Looking at me, she frowned and said, "Is that what you're wearing to work?" I nodded. Grabbing my coat, I left my lunch and walked out the door without another word. I'd only made it a few feet past the porch when my stomach again seized.

Standing back up, I swallowed hard and wiped my mouth on my sleeve. Turning, I headed down the road, smiling to think that my outfit wouldn't matter much when Mother saw her prized azalea bush.

THIRTY-SIX

The Christmas tree, small and sparsely decorated, sat in a dark corner of the room. I plugged in the strand of tiny lights, which were loosely strung on the browning and drooping branches. Long gone were the glass angels and paper Santas of our childhood, hidden with happier days.

I went into the kitchen to make a cup of tea as I tried again to settle my stomach. I quietly put the kettle on the cook stove, but before the water boiled Mother shuffled in with tired eyes and tousled hair. "Merry Christmas," I said.

She nodded as she pulled her tangled hair into a tight knot. "You too," she mumbled. I handed her a cup of tea, and we walked into the front room together.

Mother sat on the sofa cradling the cup between her palms. "It's cold in here," Mother said as she wrapped her robe more tightly around her legs.

"I could light a fire," I said.

Mother looked around as though searching for the purpose of it then said, "No. It doesn't seem worth the effort."

Pulling back the branches, I lifted out a package I'd hidden there days ago and said, "Maybe this will help."

Looking surprised, Mother set down her cup and took the gift. Pulling off the red paper, she unfolded the quilt I'd spent the last three weeks stitching.

Running her fingers over the colorful patches carefully pieced together, she said, "I always found quilting to be difficult." Admiring the work, she turned the blanket over in her hands and said, "Ms. Tarmar really did a fine job."

Taking a deep breath, I said, "Ms. Tarmar only showed me the stitches. I saved the scraps of cloth from my other sewing and quilted them together myself."

"Either way. It should be useful this winter," Mother said before pushing it aside. Picking up the tissue paper, Mother smoothed it flat and mumbled, "I didn't know we were getting gifts for each other." Setting the folded paper on the table, Mother straightened her back and said, "Besides, I think the money could've been put to better use paying bills."

I said, "Your gift didn't cost any money, Mother. Just time."

Standing, Mother said, "Yes. Well." Grabbing her teacup, she asked, "More tea?" I shook my head.

Listening to the spoon softly clink against the cup from the kitchen, I looked under the tree with no presents underneath. Sliding my hands to my still slim sides, I placed my palm over my stomach. Cradling my belly, I knew I'd already been given my gift.

THIRTY-SEVEN

The January days, dull and bleak, were bitter cold and filled with long hours of missing Samuel and not much else. I'd seen him only a few times when we happened, by chance, to pass one another on the road. Each time we stood together close and alone, I longed for it to be more than a brief moment, but Denny's words, wicked and wrong, had hollowed out a hole in my heart. I didn't believe what Denny had said but his words, like strangling weeds, had already taken root causing me to question everything.

By mid-February, I could no longer deny the ache in my heart or the swelling of my belly. So, in the cold quiet of Sunday morning, I pulled on my thickest sweater, grateful for the heavy layers that hid my own heaviness.

Stepping into the kitchen, I was careful to keep my bag in front of me as I passed Mother, who never looked up to notice. "I have some errands to run for Ms. Tarmar," I said.

"Make sure you're back in time to help with dinner," Mother said as she arranged cups in the cupboard. Grabbing an apple and my coat, I walked outside.

Standing still for a moment, I wrapped my coat tighter around me before pushing my hands deep into the pockets, protectively pressing my palms against my belly. As I carefully cradled all that was ours, I prayed that telling Samuel about the life we'd created wouldn't destroy my own.

The sun stretched across the fresh snow blanketing the cemetery. Appearing gray against the crisp snow, the tombstones stabbed through the frozen earth. The carved sentiments vanished so that the stones appeared as nothing more than perfectly piled snowdrifts. As I stood enclosed in a landscape absent of sound and people, I breathed in the raw cold.

I walked swiftly up the hill as the wind whipped up, swirling snow around my feet. Halfway up, I looked down to see only my footprints but as I rounded the top of the bank I saw other prints, large and unbroken footsteps formed from heavy boots and solid steps. I smiled, knowing they belonged to Samuel. He told me, once, that he often went to the places where he hoped to find me.

Hurrying my steps, I soon came to the small white tool shed. Quietly, I stepped beside the last footprint stopping short of the door, which was slightly open. Through the crack a thin stream of light broke across the shadow of Samuel's face. Watching him for a moment, I stood frozen. Knowing how much I loved him, I didn't mind that telling him would change our world. What I feared was that it would destroy it.

I took a deep breath and slowly opened the door wider. Hearing the creak, Samuel turned sharply. Seeing me, his face softened. "Daisy Girl," he said as he pulled me close to him. Pressing his head against mine, he whispered over and over, "I've missed you." I didn't say anything, instead I melted into him.

The shed smelled faintly of cut grass and grease, bringing back for a moment the memory of our summer spent together. Each corner was crowded with mowers, shovels, and rakes, shrinking the already small space and making moving impossible. So I stayed still wrapped in Samuel's arms until he drew back and asked, "What are you doing here?"

Reluctantly pulling my arms from him, I said, "I have to talk to you."

"Okay," Samuel said softly. He then shuffled tools from one area to the next before clearing an old workbench of a thick layer of dust and dried leaves that littered its top. Waving his hand toward it, he said, "Sit. Please." Tired from my walk and so easily worn lately, I sunk onto the bench.

Samuel stood beside an old wooden table that sat beneath the only small window. Nervously he slid his fingers across the smooth surface. I watched as the light filtering through the splintered glass cast across his cheeks before falling to the floor. As the tiny sparks of light danced upon the dark knotholes, I searched for the right words.

Samuel exhaled sharply and said, "If you're goin' do it, Daisy Girl, then just do it."

Looking up at him, I asked, "Do what?"

Turning away from me, Samuel said, "Tell me you don't want me no more."

I tried to stand but exhausted I settled back onto the bench and said softly, "Samuel, no." Staring out the window, Samuel said nothing. "Samuel, please look at me." As he slowly turned to face me, I said, "I love you, Samuel."

In one quick step, Samuel was close to me. Kneeling down, he took my hands in his and said, "I love you, Daisy Girl." Looking up at me, Samuel grinned.

"Why are you smiling?" I asked.

"Don't you see, Daisy Girl? As long as you love me ain't nothin' else matter." Serious once more, he said, "I would do anything for you."

In that moment, Samuel said the very words that made me want to tell him about the baby, but those same words also made me realize that I never could. Pulling his head onto my lap, I whispered, "I know, Samuel."

Unwilling to risk Samuel for myself or even for our baby, I said, "Denny doesn't want me to see you anymore."

Sitting up, Samuel asked, "What?"

Taking a jagged breath, I said, "Denny doesn't think we should be together."

Samuel asked, "Why?"

Putting my hand on his arm, I said, "Samuel, please. You know why."

Samuel shook my arm and said, "I do, but I want to hear you say it."

Shaking my head, I said, "No."

Leaning close to me, Samuel said, "Say it."

Looking away, I said, "I won't."

Standing abruptly, he snapped, "I'll say it."

Taking a step back, he said, "Your brother doesn't want you runnin' with a nigger, right?"

I gasped. "Samuel! No!"

Gripping the side of the table, Samuel said, "Do you think I don't know that's what white folks call me? How they see me?" Jutting out his jaw, he added, "Your brother ain't no different."

I trembled as my voice rose. "It's not what *I* see."

Samuel again crouched down in front of me and said softly, "It ain't what I see neither."

Putting his hand against my cheek, he said, "When I'm with you, Daisy Girl, all I see is love. And it ain't a color." Grabbing my hands in his, he said, "But I was fool to think that kind of seein' goes beyond the walls of that red barn."

Burying my head in his shoulder, I murmured, "You're not a fool, Samuel."

Pushing back from me, he said, "I'm a bigger fool not to see the danger in it."

Trying to pull him back to me, I said, "It could be different. We could find a way. We could—"

Samuel lightly pressed his fingers against my lips. "I love you, Daisy Girl, but we both know that there ain't no place for that kind of love in this kind of world."

Tears streamed down my face as Samuel stepped to the door. I wanted to fight it, to find a way, to pull him back to me. But knowing he was right, I dropped my head and let him walk out. As the door closed behind him, my whispered words—*I love you*—echoed off the empty walls.

Wrapping my arms tightly around myself, I tucked my chin to my chest as I rocked my body slowly back and forth. Tears streaked my cheeks as I mourned not only what I'd lost but also what I'd so easily let go.

Although I sat for only an hour more, it felt as though a lifetime had passed. Slowly standing, I left the shed and walked down the hill that rounded past Daddy's grave. Stopping for a moment, I remembered how I believed when Daddy died that God had given me a burden so heavy, I staggered under its weight. But now as I stumbled alone, with my own heaviness weighing me down, I worried this time I really would fall and no one would be there to catch me when I did.

The lock quietly clicked as I slowly turned the knob. Stepping into the dark kitchen, I was relieved that Mother wasn't home. I dropped my bag onto the table before slipping off my coat. I heard the click of the lamp right before the room lit with the glow. I gasped, startled to see Mother sitting at the table with her fingers still stretched toward the sideboard where the lamp sat.

I roughly ran my fingers across my cheeks wiping away the tears that still streamed down them. "Why were you sitting in the dark?"

Exhaling sharply, Mother snapped, "You weren't home in time for dinner."

I sighed. "I know. I'm sorry." Picking up my bag, I headed toward the hall.

Mother spun around in her seat, "Where are you going?"

Exhausted, I mumbled, "Bed."

Narrowing her eyes, Mother said, "Get back in here." She paused only a second before growling, "Now!" As I came back to the table, Mother turned back around in her chair. While I waited, she slowly stirred her tea. Then her words, staccato and sharp, sounded with each clank of her spoon tapped against the corner of her cup as she said, "Why must you always disappoint me?"

There was no answer to this question. It wasn't really a question at all. It was Mother's belief, her burden, her cross to bear. So, I said nothing. Scowling, Mother said, "You've been this way since you were a child." Shaking her head, she said, "I don't ask much of you, young lady, and still you—"

"Disappoint?" I asked.

Stopping her rant, Mother looked at me. "Come here," she said.

Stepping back, I said, "Mother, please. I'm tired."

She pushed her cup farther from her and said, "Come here." Reluctantly, I stepped toward her. Looking more closely at me, she asked, "What's wrong?" I shook my head. "Why are your eyes red and puffy?"

Turning, I said, "It's nothing. I told you. I'm tired."

Mother's moment of maternal feeling was fleeting. Sighing, she said, "Fine. Go to bed."

Reaching across the table to grab my bag, I could still feel Mother staring. "Come here," she said again. This time as I stepped closer to her, I felt uneasy. Keeping my body turned slightly from her, I said, "What?" Her brow furrowed as she took the bottom of my sweater in her hands. She pulled lightly at first before roughly tugging the material down to my legs. Then stretching it across my belly, she gasped. "Take off your sweater," she demanded.

I pulled away. "No," I said.

Standing abruptly, she shouted, "Take it off. Now!"

I pleaded, "No, Mother. Please." No longer waiting for me to obey, she pulled it over my head. Trembling, I stood before Mother. With her lips pressed tightly together, she put her hand against my swollen belly and hissed, "What is this?" Unable to say a word, my eyes welled with tears as I slowly shook my head.

Enraged, Mother swung back her arm knocking over the teacup, which crashed to the floor. Looking down, I watched as little shards of glass floated in tiny puddles of tea.

"How could you?" she screamed. Pointing her finger in my face, she shrieked, "How could you ruin us like this?" Grabbing my sweater from the floor, Mother whipped it at me and snapped, "Put it on!" Pacing between the table and me, she muttered, "I can't even look at you."

Pulling the sweater over my head, I backed against the wall. Turning sharply on her heel, Mother roughly grabbed my arm and yanked hard as she said, "Come on!" Pulling me down the hall, she raged. "I won't be ruined because of you. I won't!" Mother wrenched my arm as she shoved me into my bedroom.

She then stormed out of the room only to storm back in seconds later with a small suitcase in her hand. Throwing it onto the bed, she jerked open the latch and stomped to my dresser. "Mother, what are you doing?" Ignoring me, she tossed my clothes into the suitcase before slamming it shut.

Pulling it from the bed, she started out of the room. Panicked, I grabbed her arm. "Mother, no. What are you doing?" Following at her heels, I pleaded, "Mother, no! Please. Please." Shaking loose my grasp, she tore into the kitchen where she dropped the suitcase at the door before throwing my coat at me. Sobbing, I shook my head as I sunk to the floor. Never before had I so wanted my mother to cradle me in her arms as much as I did in that moment. Mother didn't cradle me, instead she grabbed the quilt I'd made her and shoved it toward me. "It's all you get, and it's more than you deserve." Mother's eyes never met mine as she said quietly, "A disappointment. It's all you've ever been."

I stood slowly, wiped my cheeks and picked up the suitcase before wrapping the quilt around my shoulders. I gently closed the door as I stepped outside into the cold.

Then without once looking back, I started down the road.

As I stood on his porch, I took a deep breath and knocked. Opening the door, Lizabeth, without a word, looked at me before disappearing back inside. In a moment, Denny stood in the doorway. He didn't invite me in, instead he stepped onto the porch and closed the door behind him.

Standing together quietly in the cold, I watched as Denny's gaze fell to the worn suitcase sitting at my feet. Twisting my hands together, I said, "I'm not sure what's in it. Mother packed it." Trying to smile, I said, "It could just be teacups and a party dress."

Denny didn't smile. Never taking his eyes from the suitcase, he said softly, "You can't, Birddog."

Leaning close, I tried to make him look at me before whispering, "I have nowhere else to go."

Denny turned toward the door. "You just can't," he said again.

My hand naturally slid to my stomach where a light fluttering had increased to a slow sort of rolling feeling that my own body could never dream to create, yet there it was. Placing my hand tightly against my stomach feeling the rolls quicken, I said, "Okay."

I picked up my suitcase and as my foot landed on the last step, I heard Denny whisper, "I'm sorry," before closing the door.

Taking the next step forward, I thought sadly, *So am I.*

THIRTY-EIGHT

I didn't open the door and walk in like every other day because tonight was different. Instead I knocked lightly at first and then louder until I heard her inside. Opening the door, Ms. Tarmar stood humming and smiling. Less surprised than Denny, she unwrapped the quilt from my shoulders and stepped back, inviting me in with no questions.

I stood quietly in the hall while she ran her fingers over the multi-colored patches, carefully studying each one. "You sure did a fine job. The stitches are perfect." Folding the quilt neatly into fours, she waved her hand for me to follow her upstairs. Taking me into a room down the hall from her own, she said, "It ain't been fixed up in a bit, but the room is warm and the sheets are clean."

Holding my suitcase, I slowly looked around. The walls were painted a pretty blue color like the sky after a cleansing rain. The bed, which sat in the corner next to a window draped in delicate lace curtains, looked soft and inviting. Watching me, Ms. Tarmar said, "It's an old bed, but it's comfortable." Taking blankets from a wooden storage chest, she said, "You must be exhausted." Piling my quilt on top of the blankets, she set them on the bed before setting my suitcase next to a large bureau with an oval mirror.

Opening the drawers one by one, she cleared out the knickknacks and scrap material. Giving me an uncertain smile, she said, "I'll let you settle in while I go down and heat up some soup." I nodded as Ms. Tarmar quietly closed the door. Too tired to unpack, I climbed onto the bed and pulled the blankets around me. Listening to Ms. Tarmar's soft humming trail down the stairs, I closed my eyes and quickly fell into a deep sleep.

My eyelids fluttered a few times before my eyes, bleary and tired, opened to see the last moments of the waning night. I rolled onto my back and propped the pillow beneath my head. Looking around the room in the morning light, I saw what I'd missed seeing the night before. The top of the dresser was covered in little ceramic statues of animals with a fat pink pig set in the middle. I smiled as I thought of Ms. Tarmar's pet pig and her loving nature to take in anything or anyone who needed her.

Having missed dinner last light, my stomach growled loudly. After making the bed, I changed my clothes and headed downstairs. Stepping over several sleepy cats stretched across the bottom stairs, I followed the familiar sweet smell of corn muffins.

With a bundle of sewing tucked under her arm, Ms. Tarmar carried a tray of muffins and two glasses of iced tea into the parlor room. I slowly followed behind dreading the questions I knew she'd ask. I took my usual seat and waited. Saying nothing, Ms. Tarmar simply smiled as she handed me a few shirts to mend. Taking her seat on the sofa, she took a big bite of muffin before threading her needle.

It had been a week since I'd stood scared and alone on Ms. Tarmar's porch with my suitcase and little else, yet she still asked no questions. For the past week, Ms. Tarmar treated me much the same as she had all the days I'd worked for her except that she was bit more watchful of me.

She insisted that we stopped work at three o'clock to take naps, claiming this to be her usual habit. Of course, the only nap I remembered Ms. Tarmar taking was when she'd doze on the couch midstitch, but I don't argue since most days I want to lie down long before three o'clock.

I always wake to the delicious smell of dinner, which Ms. Tarmar carefully prepares for me every day. Apart from insisting that I eat more, we don't talk much during dinner but it's a comfortable quiet. Then in the evenings, we put together puzzles or page through old catalogues together.

Every day I've spent with Ms. Tarmar, I've pushed any thoughts of Samuel far from my mind, but today I couldn't. My hands shook and my stitches slipped as every thought formed around him making the pain of missing him sharp and unsettling.

Shifting in my chair, I pulled at my shirt, which was quickly shrinking around my growing belly. Feeling Ms. Tarmar watch me, I pretended to straighten my buttons before picking up my needle. Pulling the thread through the soft cloth, I tried again to push away my thoughts of Samuel even as the life inside me reminded me of him every day.

The next morning, I lay in bed watching the dust motes dance in the wide strips of light streaming from the small window. Glancing at the clock, I got out of bed and walked slowly to the dresser. Knowing my clothes no longer fit, I reluctantly opened the top drawer. Reaching in to pull out a dress, I felt something soft brush against my leg.

I looked down to see one of my shirts hanging from the top dresser handle. I took it from the hanger and ran my fingers down the new seams studying the small stitch marks where the buttons had once been. As I pulled the newly sewn shirt over my head, it slipped comfortably over my swollen belly. Looking in the mirror, I smiled.

I walked into the parlor room already warm and sweetly scented with corn muffins. Ms. Tarmar sat on the sofa lightly rocking from side to side as she talked to the fat tabby cat at her feet. Nervously, I shifted from one foot to the other as I tried to find the right words to thank her.

Looking up at me, she smiled. I blushed. "Thank you," I said softly.

Smiling, she nodded then waved to a pile of pants near my chair. "You do the hemming today." Winking, she added,

"You keep a straight line better." I picked up a pair of pants, sat in my chair, and started to sew. Hours passed us by in the quiet purring of cats and the soft swishing of thread.

Clearing her throat, Ms. Tarmar said, "When I was a little girl, I loved to catch tadpoles, snakes, and spiders. I was always trying to make some little creature my pet." She rested her head against the back of the couch, as though leaning into the memory. Grinning, she said, "Of course, Daddy always made me let 'em go." Laughing, she added, "And most times, I did."

Pushing her sewing aside, Ms. Tarmar rested her hands in her lap. "Once I caught the most beautiful butterfly." With her fingers she outlined the shape in the air as she said, "She had big rounded blue wings and bright orange spots."

Thinking for a moment, she said, "She was just sitting on a blade of grass. She didn't fly. She just slowly flapped her wings together and apart, together and apart." Ms. Tarmar said, "Being just a kid, I was sure that her wings were clipped. So I carefully sneaked up and cupped my hands around her." Placing one hand on top of the other, Ms. Tarmar showed me her trap of folded fingers.

"I put my new pet in a mason jar." Shaking her head, she said, "I thought if I poked holes in the top, she'd be just fine. But it was such a small space that she soon stopped even fluttering her wings." Sighing, she said, "I was so worried I took her out of the jar and put her on the tip of my finger before I lightly blew on her wings. She fluttered them a few times. Slow at first, but then faster until she flew away."

Smiling, Ms. Tarmar hooked her thumbs together and waved her hands so that her fingers took flight in front of her.

Suddenly serious, she said, "My daddy always said that we can learn from even the smallest creatures." Pausing for a minute, she said, "That butterfly taught me that ain't nothing should be trapped and..." Looking at me, she said, "That nothing is as broken as it seems."

Leaning down to pet the cat that curled around her leg, she said, "As a little girl, I thought that butterfly's wings were broken, and so she needed me. But as an old lady, I know those wings weren't broken. She was just resting them, and she didn't need a push from me. She didn't need a push from no one."

Looking up at me again, she said, "She just needed to spread her wings before she could fly to where she needed to go." Ms. Tarmar stood and stretched before walking in her side-to-side sway toward me.

Standing next to my chair, she cupped her fingers under my chin and said softly, "I'm supposin' only she knew when the time was right." Smiling, she pulled back her hand and slipped quietly from the room.

THIRTY-NINE

Another week passed before I was ready to try my wings. I stood in front of the small sign scrawled with the little letters and crooked arrow pointing me once more toward Samuel's world. Only this time the warmth of summer's sun setting against the close-set houses was replaced with March's whistling winds, which gusted past knotholes and through cracks before curling into the thick syrupy mud. The recent rains had fallen heavy onto every tree, road, and house so that the air smelled of damp wood and wet soil.

This time as I stood in front of the bright purple house, there were no sheets strung on lines and no sounds of children's laughter. Instead it was strangely quiet causing me to hesitate. As I stepped onto the porch, I could feel the neighbors staring at me. Turning my head slightly, I watched as they whispered before angrily shaking their heads.

Quickly, I knocked. After three short raps, the door swung open but the woman facing me wasn't Mama. She was the young girl with the little boy who lived next door. Rolling her eyes, she pushed past me. She then shoved her arm into my side, so that I could physically feel her hatred against my skin.

Since it was Sunday, I didn't think much of someone being at Mama's house until Mama stepped into the doorway. The moment I saw her face I knew something was wrong. Her smile was gone as her laugh lines straightened into deep creases around her trembling lips. Fighting the tears that welled in her eyes, she bit her bottom lip before she choked out, "It ain't good."

Panicked, I pushed past Mama as I shouted Samuel's name. I was halfway through the kitchen when I saw him in the hallway. Running toward him, I wrapped my arms tightly around his neck, but this time it was Samuel who pulled away. Stepping back, Samuel stopped short of saying more than two words. "It's Diggs."

I lowered my head, ashamed that I never even thought of Diggs. Quietly, I asked, "What's wrong?"

Mama now stood in the kitchen where she looked into Samuel's eyes with a secret knowing. I watched as they spoke a language without words. Nodding, she slipped into the back room as Samuel said to me, "You should go."

"What happened to Diggs, Samuel?" I said as I stepped closer to him.

Clenching his jaw, he stepped back from me again and snapped, "*They* hurt him." He turned from me. Banging his fist against the wall, he said, "They beat Diggs so badly we had to carry him home." I put my hand on Samuel's shoulder as he choked back sobs. Shaking off my hand, he turned to me and said, "They didn't care that he's got the mind of a child."

Curling his lips tightly around his teeth, each word twisted through his sneer as he said, "All they cared about was he's a nigger."

"Who did this, Samuel?"

Pushing his face closer to mine, he hissed, "Who do you think?" Shaking his head, he said, "White folks who don't want a nigger running with white girl, that's who done it." Leaning against the wall, Samuel took a deep breath and said, "Neighbor said a bunch of white miners jumped him." Putting his head in his hands, he said, "I'd only left him for a bit."

"What miners?" I asked. Putting my hands on his shoulders, I demanded, "What miners, Samuel?"

He shook his head, "I don't know."

Looking into his eyes, I said, "It wasn't Denny, Samuel. It wasn't."

Pushing me from him, Samuel snapped, "Why not? He didn't want his sister loving no nigger."

My arms dropped limply to my sides. Stepping back, I stammered, "He...he wouldn't hurt anyone."

"Why are you so determined to believe that boy walks on water?" Roughly cupping my face in his hands, Samuel said, "Girl, listen to me. You're so caught up in your own grief that you can't see your brother is just a man. A man who can hate as much as he loves." Pushing his face close to mine, he said, "Maybe you seen how much Denny can love, but the bruises on my brother show how much he can hate."

Slapping hard at Samuel's hands, I jerked away and screamed, "You're wrong! You're wrong!"

Grabbing my wrists, he held on to me tightly as he shouted, "Who do you think killed my daddy?" Pushing close to me, he snapped, "Do you think angels took him?"

Lowering his voice, he said, "Do you think those men all dressed in white pushing a nigger underwater in front of his own boy was angels?"

I gasped. Stammering, I said, "Maybe...maybe..."

Samuel said, "Maybe what? Maybe he just fell? Maybe Diggs really saw angels?"

Letting go of me, Samuel stumbled back and said softly, "You should go."

I dropped my head and staggered to the door then slowly turning the knob, I walked out of his life as I walked out the door.

FORTY

Four days had passed since I had seen Samuel and Ms. Tarmar still had not asked any questions. In some ways, our time together continued unchanged. Work still ended at three o'clock for naps, but we no longer sat together in the evenings.

She put the catalogues into a drawer and an unfinished puzzle lay in pieces on the table. Now after dinner, I snuck upstairs to sit alone. Ms. Tarmar still tried to care for me by piling extra vegetables onto my plate and bringing me blankets, but she didn't smile as often or laugh as easily, and in her eyes I saw sadness when she looked at me.

After dinner, I quickly cleared the table and washed the dishes without a word before I went upstairs. I stripped my clothes from my swollen body as I looked for my nightgown, which had fallen to the floor. As I bent down to pick it up, I noticed three small crimson droplets dotting the wooden floor. Ignoring them, I thought maybe sleep would make the bleeding stop.

My eyes closed against the warmth of the sun across my face. *Summer is always so hot in this house*, I thought as I groaned. My stomach twisted in pain. Daddy warned me about eating too many cookies. I should've listened, but I loved buttercream cookies so much.

The pain was sharper now and caused me to bolt upright in bed. Wide awake now, I looked around the room, Ms. Tarmar's room. Lying back down, I took a deep breath before feeling another stab, raw and hot, to my belly. I stayed still waiting for it to pass, but the cramping only quickened. Pushing my palms against the bed, I arched my back in an effort to settle the pain, but my fingers slipped on the smooth sheet, sliding into a pool of warm, sticky liquid.

I slowly pulled my fingers from beneath the blanket. As though dipped in scarlet, blood dripped from my trembling hands. My eyes widened. Afraid, I shoved my hands back beneath the blanket and prayed, "Please, God. Please." Wrapping my arms around my belly, I pleaded, "For all that I've lost, please, God, let me have this."

Another sharp pain sliced across my stomach and back silencing my prayers. Taking another jagged breath, I focused on the pink pot-bellied pig that dug his ceramic hooves deep into the dresser until I heard a light tapping on my door. Ms. Tarmar cautiously peered through the small crack before coming in.

Taking three quick steps toward the bed, she stopped at the footboard as she carefully studied me. Sitting on the bed near my feet, she gently laid her hand lightly on my leg and said softly, "It's goin' be all right." Adjusting the blankets, she said, "I ain't ever done this myself, but I seen a lot on the farm. And it don't seem to make no matter whether it's a person or an animal." Leaning in, she said quietly, "Nature always finds a way to take care of itself."

Moving toward the door, she said, "Women are strong." Turning back to me, she added, "You're strong." Soon she was back with warm tea and kind words, but neither did much stop the pain or my fear. Sitting again on my bed, she handed me the tea. As I reached for the cup, she saw the dried blood that streaked and dotted my hands. Trying not to show her own fear, she said, "I'm goin' call Dr. Miller now."

"It's goin' be all right," she said before quickly heading out of my room. I listened as she spoke in fear-laced whispers to the doctor. With the quiet click of the phone, I felt the final cramp taking with it the sharp pain and all that I had left in my life.

Dr. Miller arrived at Ms. Tarmar's house fifteen minutes later, but time had no bearing since God had made His decision. Lifting his large wrinkled hand to my forehead, he asked, "Is the pain worse?"

I shook my head as my eyes welled with tears.

After examining me, Dr. Miller called Ms. Tarmar back into the room where she held my hand tightly as he explained. "The fetus has been completely expelled. It's not a common occurrence in this stage of pregnancy, but it happens."

Groaning softly as he picked up his medical bag, he said, "You're young and healthy. You'll recover well."

I pushed my face into the pillow. I couldn't look at the man who reduced my baby, Samuel's baby, to nothing more than an illness. It didn't matter what he said, I knew the moment my baby died that I would never recover.

Ms. Tarmar gently rubbed my hand as Dr. Miller said, "I don't want to be indelicate, but where is the fetus?" Stammering, he said, "I'm only asking because...because if you need or want...there are ways—"

Ms. Tarmar cut in, "It's been taken care of," she said as she squeezed my hand.

Dr. Miller said, "Well, good. Good."

Walking to the door, he said, "You may bleed and cramp for a while as your body rids...well, takes care of itself."

Ms. Tarmar stood. Hurrying him from the room, she said, "I'll make sure she's looked after." Leading him into the hall, she said, "I'll walk you out, Dr. Miller."

As the door closed, I lay alone with my grief, heartbroken that no one marked my baby's birth or her death. Wrapping my arms around my now empty, hollow belly, I sobbed to think that only Ms. Tarmar and I would ever know she'd lived. And even though Ms. Tarmar would also remember her short life only I would know how much it meant.

CHAPTER

FORTY-ONE

The thick clouds muted the dawn's light so that as I stood in front of the mirror my face was nothing more than sunken shadows and swollen eyes. I gripped the edge of the dresser waiting for the cramping to stop. Still holding tightly with one hand, I pulled out a dress. Slipping it over my head, the cotton slid over my still swollen belly. Looking down, I winced to think of its emptiness.

With slow, steady steps I made my way to the bed where I sat for a moment. I swallowed hard, forcing the bile in my throat back into my stomach before taking a deep breath. Sliding carefully off of the bed, I turned and sank onto my knees. Lifting up the ends of the blankets, I reached underneath the bed. I blindly ran my fingers across the dusty cold floor until I found it. Grasping tightly, I pulled out the box.

Leaning against the bed, I cradled the small brown box in my arms as I'd cradled my belly only days before. I lovingly ran my fingers across the smooth cardboard in soft strokes. I didn't open the box. I didn't need to open it. I knew what lay inside, quiet and small. She looked like a tiny kitten wet with blood and fluid but she was perfectly formed, and she was mine. She was Samuel's and mine.

I gently tucked the box under my arm and went downstairs where Ms. Tarmar sat sipping her tea as she did every Saturday morning. Seeing me, she set the cup down. We looked at one another for a moment before she glanced at the box, smiled, and nodded.

I knew Ms. Tarmar was right. After all, she'd been right about the box. She was the one who suggested the small but sturdy shoebox when she came in and found us, bloodstained and helpless. And she was right about what I had to do. So quietly, I closed the door behind me before starting down the road to bury my baby.

The day was a dull gray as heavy clouds hung low in the sky. The recent heavy rains caused mud to splatter onto my shoes as I slowly shuffled my feet. Still in pain, I could only take so many steps before I had to stop. Feeling the familiar stab, my body pitched forward. My fingers whitened as I gripped the box harder waiting for it to be over. Taking a jagged breath, I again started down the road.

I walked until I saw them. The curly-haired and smooth-skinned cherubs perched high on the wooden gate. Carved with wide, innocent eyes, they seemed to watch as I walked by the cemetery. Pausing for a moment, I considered going to him. To sit where I had sat all the other times that I'd grieved. But today wasn't about my pain. It was about my daughter and her right to a proper goodbye.

With the box tucked underneath my arm, I continued walking. I wondered if I passed a stranger what they would think. Would they see the box and believe that I'd just bought shoes to match a dress? I wished it were true. I wished I were just a young girl with a pretty pair of shoes.

Pushing back the soft pine branches, I inhaled the familiar scent of damp earth and fallen leaves. Comforted, I pushed forward until I reached the creek. The rich, dark smell swelled over the branches of the willows seeping into the bark, the water, and the brush until I could taste it.

I slowly tilted my head up guiding my eyes over the trunk's wrinkled brown skin and up into the tree's flowing locks of delicate tear-shaped leaves to the slender limbs bent to the ground, weeping. Staring into the circle of secret grief the bowed limbs created, I remembered Samuel's words. And then I knew I had to bury her in a place she'd always be mourned even when I could no longer weep for her.

I set the box gently on the ground, then I kneeled beside my baby and started to dig. Clawing at the unrelenting earth, I searched for a sharp stone. Finding one, I stabbed it into the hard ground over and over until finally the dirt released. Pushing my fingers into the small cracks I'd made, I pulled and scraped until I'd hollowed out a small hole.

Pulling back my hands, mud-stained and cut, I picked up the box and pressed it close to my chest. "I love you," I whispered as my tears tapped upon the box. Wiping dry the drops, I smoothed the top with my hands before placing into the ground. Sprinkling the dirt on top of the soft cardboard, I said what I believed would be impossible—goodbye.

I'd only taken a few steps when I heard the sound of twigs snapping beneath footsteps. I turned to see him standing not far from me. I didn't know how he knew or why he was here. I only cared that he was. Without a word, he stepped close to me. Taking my mud-stained hand in his, he pulled me to him. Grateful, I sunk into his shoulder and sobbed.

Patiently he waited, then gently pushing me back from him, he pulled a worn red handkerchief from his pocket and wiped my cheeks. From his other pocket, he pulled a small hand-carved wooden cross, which he sunk deep into the soft mound of dirt on my baby's grave.

He slowly rose to his feet and turned toward me, but he didn't wrap his arms around me. He didn't tell me it would be all right. Instead, he stood silent for a moment before he said quietly, "I'm sorry, Birddog." As he turned and walked away, I knew I would never see Denny again.

Abandoned and alone in my grief, it felt as though my soul split into a thousand splintered pieces. Sorrow seemed to spread over the trees, the ground, and me until I felt surrounded by pain causing happiness and hope to break and fall far from me. And in the shattered spaces a new me—vacant and empty—emerged.

CHAPTER

FORTY-TWO

I turned my hand slightly so that the tiny tear slowly slipped across my skin, resting for a moment in the deep crease of my palm before lightly landing on my daughter's arm.

The droplet quietly coursed across her dirt-stained skin before taking its final fall into the soft soil.

As she slipped slowly back from her memories, I asked, "Mother, are you okay?"

Seeming uncertain, she nodded then asked, "Where were you?"

I mumbled, "I was in the woods."

Staring past me, she said, "You're always in the woods. Why?"

I shrugged. Looking at me, she said, "You're never home now that he's gone." I looked away. "Why?" she asked.

I didn't answer. When she raised her arm, I flinched. Pulling her hand back to her side, she asked, "Are you afraid of me?"

I said, "No." Lowering my head, I said, "Sometimes."

I expected her to be angry, to demand why, instead she said quietly, "I'm sorry." Surprised, I said nothing. "I was afraid of my mother sometimes too," she admitted.

"I was her greatest disappointment," she said. "And she was mine." Cupping her fingers beneath my chin, she raised my eyes to meet hers. "Am I *your* disappointment?" I shook my head. She sighed. "I don't want to be."

Staring past me again, she said, "My daddy once told me that we all make our own cages in this life from some decision or another until we're trapped." As her eyes welled with tears, she said, "Maybe that's what happened to me. I ended up in a cage that I made. Not knowing how I got in or how to get out." Looking at me, she said, "I trapped myself but even worse I trapped you in here with me."

We stood silently together for a long time before Mother said, "Come on. I want you to meet someone." Without any other explanation, Mother started toward the road with me close behind. She walked with determination as I followed with curiosity until we made our way to Calvers Creek. The humid air clung to our skin and slowed our breathing in time to our measured steps until she suddenly stopped.

Standing in front of a weeping willow tree with a crown that crested above all the others, she said, "We're here." As though pulling back a curtain, she parted the slender branches that cascaded across the downy grass. Nodding at me to come inside, she followed behind before releasing the long-limped drapery around us.

Kneeling, she pulled weeds from the base of the trunk and smoothed the dirt into circles with a motherly tenderness she'd rarely shown me. As I watched her, I saw only dirt and untamed grass until she said, "She was my first." Reaching her hand to me, she pulled me next to her and said, "She died a long time ago." Pulling up another weed, she said, "And a part of my heart died with her."

"I'm sorry," I whispered. As she looked at me, I said, "I'm sorry you've been sad for so long."

Taking my hand into her own, she said, "I don't want to be anymore." Squeezing my hand gently, she said, "Coming here today with you reminded me that I'm lucky." She smiled. "I have you and..." Glancing toward her baby's grave, she said, "I had her."

Shaking my head, I said, "But her death made you so sad."

"It did, but a wise and kind woman once told me that we don't know real hurt until we know real love." Mother stood and parted the branches. Stepping out, she allowed the curtain of tear-shaped leaves to drape around her grief once more.

By the time we reached the road, dusk had fallen casting scarlet strips across the sky. Looking up, Mother said, "That same wise woman told me that red is the color of rage and shame." Smiling, she said, "But it's also the color of passion and love." Mother stopped. Her smile slipped as she said,

"Your daddy isn't coming home." I could feel my eyes well with tears as she said kindly, "But we are going to be okay."

With a new tenderness, she brushed a tear from my cheek and said, "Sometimes we can't cry enough for all the pain we feel." Pulling me to her, she wrapped her arms around me and whispered, "So, we let the willows weep." I nodded and together we walked forward, away from the grief and toward a life that hopefully held a little less hurt.

ACKNOWLEDGMENTS

Thank you to my editor, Victoria Hughes-Williams, for her well-constructed and invaluable feedback on my manuscript. I appreciated her keen eye to what structurally worked within my novel while still helping me to maintain my creative voice throughout the work.

Thank you to my proofreader, Beth Attwood, for her attention to detail in making sure that not one comma was missed or one word out of place.

Thank you to my designer, Sarah Beaudin, for her beautifully artistic cover design and her meticulous styling of the manuscript layout.

I also want to thank my marketing consultant, Elizabeth Psaltis, for her ongoing commitment and effort to ensuring that *Let the Willows Weep* finds a readership who will love to read this book as much as I have loved writing it. Her advice and guidance have been invaluable, and I am grateful to work with someone whose expertise is helping my book to find its place in the world.

Made in the USA
Coppell, TX
05 August 2024

35631076R10163